HOW TO UNDO
THE PROUD
BILLIONAIRE

HOW TO UNDO THE PROUD BILLIONAIRE

JOSS WOOD

MILLS & BOON

First published in Great Britain 2020
by Mills & Boon, an imprint of HarperCollins*Publishers*
1 London Bridge Street, London, SE1 9GF
www.harpercollins.co.uk

HarperCollins*Publishers*
1st Floor, Watermarque Building,
Ringsend Road, Dublin 4, Ireland

Large Print edition 2021

© 2020 Joss Wood

ISBN: 978-0-263-28854-4

Printed and bound in Great Britain
by CPI Group (UK) Ltd, Croydon, CR0 4YY

CHAPTER ONE

"YOUR PHONE IS RINGING."

In his expansive corner office on the top floor of their company headquarters, Radd Tempest-Vane pulled his attention off the report in his hand, his eyes bouncing from his brother's face to his smartphone, just released to the market, half-buried by a pile of reports. He pulled it free, cursed when papers fell to the expensive carpeting and turned the phone to show Digby the screen.

"Naledi Radebe." Frustration jumped into Digby's navy blue eyes, so like Radd's own. They had been born eleven months apart and had on occasion been mistaken for twins. All three Tempest-Vane brothers shared the same dark brown hair, deep blue eyes and six-foot-plus height. Radd ignored the suddenly tight grip on his heart. So much time had passed, but sometimes he still thought of Jack in the present tense.

He probably always would.

"Are you going to answer her call?" Digby asked from the sleek leather couch next to Radd's desk, his eyes already back on the screen of the laptop resting on his knees. Every few weeks, depending on their schedules, he and Digby met—either here or at Digby's equally luxurious office at The Vane—to strategize, plan and discuss supersensitive, for-their-eyes-only company information.

"No, I'm busy. All the arrangements for her wedding to Johnathan Wolfe have been finalized and he's happy."

Radd returned his attention to his laptop. He didn't have time to deal with the attention-seeking socialite today. The last time he checked, he and his brother had a massive international empire to run, deals to make, new markets to conquer.

An empire to restore to its former glory, a family name to rehabilitate and a multi-billion-dollar deal to protect.

Beyond the floor-to-ceiling bank of electrochromic glass was an extraordinary view of Table Mountain and the endlessly fascinating Atlantic Ocean seaboard. If he was in the habit of looking out of the window, Radd might've noticed that it was a perfect day to spend on the beach or, at the very least, outside.

But Radd's attention never strayed far from business so, instead of looking at his stunning view, his eyes flicked over to the massive electronic screen on the wall opposite him to look at the changes he'd made on the complicated spreadsheet they were working on. Something looked off with the figures; he'd made a mistake somewhere. Radd gritted his teeth and scraped his hand over his face, trying to wipe away his frustration. He wasn't in the habit of making unforced errors, and wasting time upped his annoyance levels.

His phone jangled and, once again, he let the call go to voice mail.

"It's your fault for agreeing to play wedding planner," Digby commented.

"Naledi thinks that because her father tied the purchase of the mine to her wedding, she can boss me about. Dammit, I'm far too busy to play wedding planner," Radd growled.

"And too rich and too important..." Digby mocked him.

Dig was the only one allowed to tease him, and nobody could cut him down to size quicker than his silver-tongued sibling.

Radd was more acerbic, impatient and abrupt than his brother. A previous lover once called him robotic and, had he cared enough to respond—he hadn't—he might've agreed with her assessment. Feelings were messy, prickly and uncomfortable, and thanks to his narcissistic parents and his brother Jack's death, he'd cultivated an attitude of stoicism, training himself not to react, to get perturbed, upset or excited.

Though, knowing he was a week away from acquiring the mine almost tempted his habitually unemotional heart to flutter.

Initially, it had been Jack's burning ambition to rebuild the Tempest-Vane group of companies; he'd been almost evangelical in his quest to restore respect to the family name. For generations, their ancestors had been on the right side of history and people from all walks of life had known that, despite their immense wealth, the Tempest-Vanes stood for equality, freedom and tolerance.

Then the businesses and assets fell into

their father's hands and the Tempest-Vane name became synonymous with excess, dissipation, laziness and entitlement. And all those excesses had been splashed on the front pages of tabloids, locally and internationally.

It was hard enough to be the child of celebrity parents, but it had been hell being the sons of Gil and Zia Tempest-Vane.

Radd leaned back in his chair and closed his eyes, remembering the humiliation he had felt every time a scandal hit the papers. Jack, as the eldest, frequently took them to task, but Gil and Zia ignored his pleas to calm down, to stay out of the news. And then they stopped taking his calls or replying to his emails.

None of the brothers were particularly surprised when their parents' lackadaisical efforts to stay in touch dwindled to infrequent text messages and once-a-year, if they were lucky, visits.

Then Jack died and their parents' behavior—before, during and after the funeral—was the final straw.

Although their escapades still hit the gossip columns with alarming and irritating frequency, years passed with no contact between them. Then, a year and some months ago, Radd received an email from his father, demanding a meeting with his sons. They were coming home, and there was someone they wanted them to meet…

The next news they had of their parents was of their deaths; Gil and Zia's car had left the road in Southern California and crashed into the sea below. Radd still wondered who was so important to his parents that they were prepared to reach out and break the almost twenty-year silence.

He had a vague theory, but no proof to back it up.

Radd sighed, glanced at the spreadsheet and was reminded of what they were doing and why. He'd been sixteen when he realized all the family businesses were gone, along with most of the once-impressive Tempest-Vane fortune. Somehow, his parents had not only managed to strip the company of its most valuable assets, but also spend a good portion of the proceeds of the sales. The rest they had squirreled into untouchable trusts.

And they'd managed to do it on the q.t. To this day, Radd abhorred secrets and surprises.

Now, thanks to a little luck and lots of sweat—he didn't do tears—the ranch and The Vane, the beloved Cape Town icon and the hotel Digby so loved, were back under their ownership.

But the final contract had yet to be signed, and Vincent Radebe, the current owner of the diamond mine they were trying to reacquire, and his demanding daughter stood between them and their end goal. The Sowetan-based businessman hadn't been shy about tacking on some nonbusiness-related demands. His youngest child, and only daughter, was recently engaged and he was determined to give her the wedding of her dreams.

Because the Tempest-Vane brothers owned the most exclusive and sophisticated hotel and wedding venue in Cape Town, Vincent wanted the reception to be held at The Vane. Vincent also demanded Radd accommodate the wedding party at Kagiso Ranch, their six-star, phenomenally exclusive game reserve, for the week leading up to the wedding. All at cost.

Frustratingly, Radd could only find an opening for both venues eight months after his and Vincent's initial discussion, thus delaying the sale. They couldn't launch the extensive PR campaign, and the rebranding of the Tempest-Vane group of companies—reassociating their surname with corporate social responsibility and social justice instead of their parent's wild life, dissoluteness and licentiousness—until they owned the mine.

Radd's low store of patience had run out seven and a half months ago.

His phone rang again, and Radd snatched it up, thoroughly annoyed. "Naledi, what's the problem?"

"Radd, my life is ruined!" Naledi wailed. Radd rolled his eyes as he put his phone on speaker. "Everything is falling apart!"

"Of course her life is tough, she only received twenty-one million on her twenty-first birthday," Digby murmured, loud enough for Radd, but not Naledi, to hear.

Radd knew what Digby was thinking: when they were twenty-one and twenty-two, they'd ceased all contact with their dysfunctional and narcissistic parents and the only cash they had had access to was in a trust fund set up by their grandfather to pay for their education. Luckily, Gray Tempest-Vane vastly overestimated the amount needed to pay for their education and they'd taken every extra cent they had had and invested in a tech company developing a new type of payment system for internet transactions.

One small online retailer had picked up their system, then another and then they had landed Yours!, one of the three biggest online retailers in the world. The offers to buy them out had started rolling in and, five years ago, they had sold the company to a tech giant, and Radd and Digby had become two of the youngest billionaires in the world. Still, certain financial doors remained closed, thanks to their father's legacy of defaulting on loans and being economical with the truth. Vincent Radebe was a case in point, but they'd persisted.

Radd intended to change the collective mindset of the old school captains of commerce and industry.

"What's the problem, Naledi?" Radd demanded, gripping the bridge of his nose between his thumb and forefinger.

"The flowers have arrived at Kagiso Lodge…"

"And?" Radd asked, eyeing the mountain of work he needed to plough through before the end of the weekend. Because life was currently finding it fun to screw with him, Vincent wanted him to host the pre-wedding party so, the first thing on Monday morning, he was flying to Kagiso Lodge.

Just shoot him now.

"The flowers are there, but my florist isn't! She's had the gall to schedule an operation for appendicitis."

"What do you want me to do about it, Naledi?"

"Find me another florist, Radd," Naledi demanded in her breathy, baby-doll voice. Radd wasn't fooled; Naledi was her father's daughter and below her gorgeous surface resided a band of tungsten, a hard layer of give-me-what-I-want-now.

Jesus wept. Radd was worth over a billion dollars and he'd been reduced to asking "How high?" when the Radebes said "Jump." Normally, he was the one who issued orders, who expected to be obeyed, who made demands and expected others to work their asses off to give him what he wanted before he wanted it.

The ill-fitting, uncomfortable shoe was on the other foot, and Radd didn't care for the sensation.

"The staff at the lodge have all taken flower arranging courses, Naledi," Digby interjected in a reasonable tone. He mimed putting a gun to his head and pulling the trigger.

"I will *not* settle for less than the best!"

"Then we'll most definitely find you a florist and we'll make sure they are at the ranch tonight," Digby told her, sounding ridiculously reasonable. Radd sent him a heated *What the hell?* look, and Digby mimed the word *Mine*. Then, in case Radd didn't catch his meaning the first time, he mimed the word again.

Right. Gotcha.

After agreeing to find Naledi a florist, Radd disconnected his call, immediately pulled up another number and impatiently waited for his assistant to answer his call.

As briefly as possible, he told Andrew what

he wanted. "Find me a florist, get them to meet me at the office at two-thirty. I'll fly them to Kagiso tonight and return them to Cape Town when they're done. It shouldn't take more than a day."

"Rate?" Andrew asked.

"I don't care, just get me someone good."

Radd disconnected and looked longingly at the state-of-the-art coffee machine on the far side of the room. Normally Andrew provided him with a steady supply of caffeine but, since the offices were empty, as he and Digby were discussing sensitive corporate and financial matters, it was self-serve. And, somehow, despite both of them having above-average IQs and post-graduate degrees in business, neither he nor Digby could make a decent cup of coffee.

Radd tried to ignore the headache building behind his eyes. "Andrew will work on the florist problem."

"I doubt he's going to find a celebrity florist who'll drop everything to fly to Kagiso at a moment's notice."

Radd wasn't so sure. Despite being a relentless pain in his ass, the Radebes were an influential African family, and working for them would add cachet to anyone's resume. Kagiso Ranch was also one of most exclusive safari destinations in the world and, while they tried to fly under the radar, he and Digby were two of the country's richest, and therefore most eligible, bachelors. Between them and the Radebes, there was serious name recognition.

Digby nodded, rolled his shoulders and pulled his laptop toward him. "Well, there's nothing we can do until then."

Radd looked at his watch, a vintage Rolex Daytona, one of only a few in the world. It had been his grandfather's, then Jack's, and it was his most prized possession. He set a mental alarm. Three hours had to be more than enough time for Andrew to find someone because, really...

How difficult could it be to toss some flowers into a vase?

Brinley Riddell noticed a Porsche Cayenne reversing out of a parking space right in front of the path leading to the beach and swung her nineteen-sixties Beetle Betsy into the spot, ignoring the angry hoots of the driver she'd cut off.

You snooze, you lose.

As she yanked up her handbrake and pulled the key from the ignition, her cell phone buzzed with an incoming message. Seeing her best friend's profile picture on her screen, she swiped her screen to read the message.

What are you doing tonight and tomorrow?

Was that a trick question?

I'm dining with Bradley Cooper tonight and brunching with Oprah at The Vane at nine.

Brinley grinned at her facetious reply. She and Abby, friends since school, shared a small cottage in Bo Kaap, and Abby knew reading was Brin's favorite way to spend a Saturday night.

Abby, the queen of Cape Town's clubbing scene, replied with a short, pithy sentence and a couple of rolling eye emojis.

You've got to get a life, Brin. Good thing I'm here to make that happen.

Brin didn't reply because a) she wanted to get to the beach, and b) they'd had this argument a hundred times before. Brin was very happy to spend the evening alone, while Abby needed people and attention like she needed air to breathe. In that way she was very much like Brin's influencer, socialite sister Kerry, but, thankfully, in every other way that was important, she wasn't.

She wasn't rude or mean or self-absorbed or selfish. Abby liked men but, unlike Brin's half sister, she didn't use or play games with them. Abby wasn't high maintenance.

In a smooth, much-practiced movement, Brin shoved her hand through the open window and grabbed the outside handle to open her door. None of her car doors locked but, by some miracle, her car had yet to land in a chop shop. Maybe it was the bright pink-and-rust color or maybe car thieves had standards, but so far, so good.

Slamming her car door shut, Brinley stepped onto the pavement and pushed her soft, loose curls off her face. It was one of those perfect African days. The summer sun was high in the sky but a soft wind kept the temperature from being unbearable. Standing at the top of the steep set of stairs leading to the beach, she smiled, struck as she always was by the beauty of the white sand and turquoise water. This was one of her favorite beaches and, since moving to Cape Town six months ago, she'd spent many of her free days down here, swimming, reading and, because she could, ogling the hot surfers and the volleyball players.

Looking was always fun, but Brin had a strict "Look, don't engage" policy. When she'd left Johannesburg, she'd promised herself that she'd give herself all the time she needed to find herself, to discover who she was and what she stood for…

She was a very messy work in progress and dating added complications she didn't need. And men weren't, let's be honest here, anywhere as satisfying as coffee, chocolate or bacon.

Brin leaned her butt against the door of her car and tipped her face to the sun, loving the gentle heat on her skin. She pulled in a series of deep breaths, telling herself that there was no need to rush, that she was allowed to stand still, to take a breath and to take the moment.

There were no emails to answer, text messages to look at, a demanding sister/boss to run after, people to please. It had taken all her strength and a great deal of courage to walk away from her dominating mother and sister, and she constantly reminded herself that she no longer answered to anyone and was a free agent…or she was trying to be.

God, leaving them had been the one and only thing she'd ever done for herself and by herself, and had she not, she would've lost herself forever. It had been so damn close…

Brin stared out to sea, trying and failing to remember a time when Kerry's wants, needs and ambitions weren't crucially important. Their family revolved around her half sister, and Brin might have still been in Johannesburg, working as Kerry's very underappreciated personal assistant, had she not caught *her* sister kissing *her* boyfriend.

As long as lived she'd never forget their glib, unremorseful responses.

"Look, let's be honest here. Your sister is smarter, incredibly successful and so much

sexier than you. What was I supposed to say when she suggested we hook up...no?"

Well, Malcolm, yes.

Kerry's eyes had held malice as she had twisted the knife of betrayal. *"And, darling, don't you think that you are punching above your weight with Malcolm?"*

Strangely, Kerry's betrayal and her mother's reaction to the situation hurt far more than discovering Malcolm was a cheating jerk. On hearing about their fight, their mom instantly dismissed Brin's feelings and, without hesitation or thought, defended Kerry's actions, reminding her that her half sister was special, that she should be given a pass because she was beautiful and super famous. And really, who could blame Malcolm for choosing Kerry over her?

Everyone did. And always would.

Standing there, feeling slapped by her mother's dismissive words, being told she was overreacting, Brin knew she needed to leave, to run, as hard and as fast as she could.

By the next morning she was in Cape Town and, so far, she'd resisted their constant pleas, demands and manipulations to return home because, deep down, she knew her only role was to make their lives easier.

She'd swapped her garden flat for a tiny second bedroom in Abby's house, the use of Kerry's Benz for wheezy Betsy, and her waitressing job barely covered her bills. But she was free of criticism, of being micromanaged, of standing in her sister's very long shadow. In Cape Town, she could breathe.

She could be Brin.

That was, if she lasted in Cape Town. Brin thought about her depleted bank account and rubbed the back of her neck. She'd picked up a couple of gigs doing floral designs to supplement the money she earned from waitressing, but living in Cape Town was pricey and her expenses far outstripped her income. Her savings were depleted and, if something didn't change soon, she was heading for trouble.

Might-have-to-go-home or ask-my-family-for-a loan trouble. *Bleurgh.*

About to walk down the steps, Brin heard the low rumble of an expensive car and watched as a deep red supercar swung into the parking lot. This was Clifton, one of the wealthiest parts of the country, so seeing seriously expensive cars wasn't a novelty, but this was a James Bond car: glamorous, powerful and just a little, or a lot, dangerous.

And sexy. Brin was surprised to see the beast slide into the just-vacated parking spot next to hers. It was a beautiful machine, but not her style. She'd be terrified to drive it, thinking that the smallest scratch would cost her a few years' salary to fix.

Who needed that sort of pressure? Betsy got her, wheezing and spluttering, where she needed to go.

Brin felt the heat from the pavement burning through her cheap flip-flops, the heat of the sun on her bare shoulders. She couldn't wait to dive into the water; she was in desperate need of some Vitamin Sea.

"Brinley Riddell?"

Brinley slowly turned at the deep, growly voice and saw the driver of the supercar looking at her. He was tall, broad and whip-her-breath-away good-looking. Brin sighed when he rested his thick arms on the car roof, his big biceps pulling the fabric of his shirt against his skin.

Hot, hot, hot. And...kill me now.

Unlike his brother, Radd Tempest-Vane stayed out of the gossip columns, but Brin instantly recognized the city's sexiest and most elusive bachelor billionaire. He was even better looking, if that was at all possible, than the photos she'd see of him in magazines and online. His wavy hair was, in real life, a deep, rich brown, his face more angles and planes, and his mouth a great deal grimmer than she remembered. And those eyes, God, his eyes...

Navy blue most would call them. But, to Brinley, they were the color of the inside of a blue pansy or the deep, dark shade of blue delphiniums. They were eyes holding a thousand secrets...

Her knees a little soft, Brin leaned back against Betsy as he approached her, idly wondering what the hell Radd Tempest-Vane, her best friend's boss's boss, was doing here at two-thirty in the afternoon. Since he was dressed in casual chinos and an untucked white button-down shirt with the sleeves rolled up, tanned arms corded with muscle on display, she presumed he wasn't headed for the beach.

His body was staggering, all leashed power and feline grace. When their eyes connected, fireworks exploded on her skin and, deep inside, her womb throbbed, wanting or needing some intangible thing—unexplainable, unfamiliar.

"You are Brinley Riddell?" Radd demanded as he approached her.

He was here because he was looking for her. Brin swallowed and swallowed again. Why?

"Yes, I'm Brin," Brin said, watching as he echoed her stance and leaned his butt against his car, facing her. He pushed his hands into the pockets of his pants, his expression inscrutable.

"My name is Radd Tempest-Vane."

They both knew that she knew who he was, so Brin wasn't sure why he bothered to introduce himself.

"I know." Brin yanked her eyes off him and gestured to his car. "Nice car," she said, wanting to break the silence between them. "What is it?"

"Aston Martin DBS Superleggera," Radd curtly replied, his eyes not leaving her face. She felt pinned to the tarmac, unable to move.

Her stomach whirled and swirled, and all the moisture from her mouth disappeared. She wondered whether his mouth would soften when he kissed her, how his hands would feel on her naked skin. Brinley just knew that Radd was the type of guy who could give her everything she needed sexually and a great deal of what she never knew she wanted.

So this was what sexual chemistry felt like…

If Malcolm was out of your league, sister dear, then Radd Tempest-Vane inhabits a galaxy far, far away. He's dated A-list Hollywood celebrities, international supermodels and, on occasion, a princess or two.

Brin did not appreciate hearing Kerry's voice in her head and she silently cursed. She was not going to build him up into some mythical creature just because he was crazy-rich, famous and lava-hot. It was a sure bet that Radd, like her sister, was another bright spotlight, drawing energy from those around him to shine.

It's just attraction, Brin reminded herself, *a biological urge.* It didn't mean *anything...* she wouldn't let it.

Brin gave herself a mental slap and ordered her body to return some blood to her head so she could think. When she felt like she could construct a proper sentence, she pushed her sunglasses into her hair and lifted her chin. "You know my name and you aren't dressed for an afternoon on the beach, so I presume you are here, looking for me."

"I am." Radd nodded but didn't elaborate.

Okay, was she going to have to have to pull teeth to get him to explain? "Would you like to tell me why?"

Because, honestly, she had no idea what Africa's sexiest billionaire could want with her. Unlike her sister, she was neither bold nor beautiful. She didn't socialize in the same circles he did; hell, she didn't socialize at all. She was everything he wasn't: run-of-the-mill, down-to-earth, habitually penniless.

Brin saw something flash in his eyes, an emotion she didn't recognize. Confusion? Surprise? If he hadn't been Radd Tempest-Vane, with a reputation for being ruthless, cucumber-cool and hard as a rock, she might've thought he was feeling a little off-balance.

No, she was just projecting her feelings onto him. After all, being tracked down by a billionaire at the beach was something that happened in romance novels, not to ordinary girls living ordinary lives. From what she knew of him, and it wasn't much, this Tempest-Vane brother was tough and determined, a prime example of an alpha male who didn't suffer fools. He had a reputation for going after what he wanted and not stopping until he achieved his goal. He was shrewd, powerful and intimidating.

"My PA has spent most of the morning trying to find me a florist to do some arrangements at my ranch before a wedding party arrives midmorning Monday. He was not successful in his quest to find me a celebrity florist at short notice," Radd said, his tone businesslike.

Brin wasn't surprised. It was the end of spring, and the wet and dismal Cape weather had retreated, leaving warm days and cooler nights. It was a busy time for functions, parties and weddings.

"After being unsuccessful at reaching anyone, my assistant called his assistant for help, and she *suggested you.*"

God bless Abby, Brin thought. "You need a floral designer?"

Radd gave her a try-to-keep-up look. Along with gorgeous and ripped, he was arrogant, too.

Fabulous.

But if he was offering work, she'd jump at his offer, any offer. All she needed was an idea of what the client wanted, the flowers—obviously—and supplies. She was good at what she did, she just needed a chance to prove it. And doing work for a Tempest-Vane brother, or for one of his companies, would be a bright, shiny gold star on her résumé.

And, as a bonus, her bank would stop sending her you-are-low-on-funds reminders.

"I can help you," Brin told him, trying to not to sound too eager. "When do you need me to start, where must I be and how much are you going to pay me?"

"Now, at Kagiso Ranch and twenty-five thousand."

Right. Well. Brin placed her hand on Betsy to stabilize herself.

Holy damn, Superman.

CHAPTER TWO

RADD'S FINGERTIPS DUG into his biceps and it took every bit of determination he possessed to keep his tongue behind his teeth.

Because Brinley Riddell was drop-dead stunning.

Radd pulled in a deep breath, then another, trying to ignore his racing heart and the fact his pants were a size smaller across the crotch than they'd been ten minutes before. He looked around, desperately looking for an alternative explanation for his racing heart and why his nerve endings were on fire.

Maybe he was getting sick, but that wasn't likely since he was super fit, took vitamins and was as healthy as a horse. No, it was because this woman had the power to drop him to his knees…and that was crazy. He was clearly losing his mind.

He liked women and women liked him back, but he'd never been the type to allow any female to rob him of his breath, or his ability to speak.

Brinley Riddell, damn her, had come closer than most.

Radd dropped his sunglasses over his eyes and, while she took in his job offer, allowed himself the immense pleasure of looking at her from behind his mirrored shades.

She was the embodiment of a rainbow-nation child, a variety of races and mixed genes. Her skin was a rich, luscious creamy light brown, her cheekbones were high and sharp, and her mouth was wide, sensuous and made to be kissed. Her hair was a tumble of long, loose, dark curls and, he'd bet his car, soft to the touch.

She was tall for a woman, five eight or five nine, but he still had five or six inches on her. Her tiny denim shorts showed off long and shapely legs, and the wind occasionally lifted her loose vest, allowing him glimpses of spectacular breasts under two orange-colored triangles. Her stomach was as flat as a board, but he'd caught a glimpse of her ass as he'd pulled into the parking area and it was, yeah, stunning.

She was possibly the most attractive woman he'd met in a long, long time. And if he hadn't been in such a bind, he'd walk away right now. It didn't happen often, but when he met a woman who could impact his life, he always, always left.

He liked sex, had it as often as he could—which hadn't been too often lately, thanks to his workload—but he chose his partners carefully. They were always attractive, knew not to talk to the press and, most importantly, they accepted he wasn't interested in anything more than a few hours of mutually shared pleasure.

And, crucially, they didn't make him feel anything beyond the normal drive for sexual fulfillment. After being tainted, teased and tormented by the gossip generated by his parents crazy-ass lifestyle and escapades—up until their death he'd lived his life on a knife-edge waiting for the next story to break or shoe to fall, another scandal to slap him sideways—he'd decided, years ago, to not only live his life out of the limelight, but to do it solo. He could control his words, actions and choices, but not anyone else's.

Also, critically, casual affairs allowed him to remain emotionally numb and, after spending the part of his life coping with his unstable and narcissistic parents and then dealing with Jack's death, he and Numb were comfortable companions.

And, it was proven, relationships brought surprises, and surprises were something he could, without a doubt, live without.

Radd pulled his thoughts back to what was important. He needed to get Brinley to agree to fly to Kagiso with him this afternoon and to make—he'd checked—an arrangement for the lobby, two for the long dining table, one for the veranda and more than a dozen smaller arrangements, one for each of the guest's beds and bathrooms.

"It's a tall order, but the original florist committed to the time frame, so it's doable." Radd finished his explanation, searching Brinley's face for a reaction. When she just stared at him, he rubbed the back of his neck again. "Is it doable?"

Brinley held up her hand, silently asking him to slow down. He'd give her a minute to catch up, but they were running out of time, dammit. They had to be at the airport in forty-five minutes, and it was, even in the Aston, a thirty-minute drive.

Knowing they were short on time, he'd arranged for Abigail to return to the home she shared with Brinley and pack her a bag, then drive to the airport to leave it with his air steward. If Brinley said yes, and he had no intention of letting her say no, they would leave for the airport immediately.

"Well?"

"Twenty-five grand?" Brinley whispered. "And I'll be back in Cape Town tomorrow night?"

"I'll go to thirty if you make up your mind in the next minute," Radd stated, impatient.

Two dimples appeared as her mouth widened into a smile, and he felt like she'd slammed a battering ram into his solar plexus. God, that smile should be registered as a dangerous weapon.

"Deal," Brinley said. "But I need to go home, shower and change, and pack a bag."

"Your friend is packing a bag for you and she will deliver it to the airport. You can shower and change on my plane, but we're leaving now," Radd said, standing up straight. He had her agreement, excellent. Now all he had to do was keep his hands off her for twenty-four, twenty-five hours.

Surely, he could do that?

Brinley didn't move from her position. "Wow, you certainly don't waste time."

"I know what I want and I know how to get it," Radd replied, sounding edgy. *Tough*.

Brinley lifted a stubborn chin and patted her crappy car. "I'm not leaving Betsy here."

He didn't understand why people named their cars—it was stupidly sentimental and frankly ridiculous—but, strangely, the old-fashioned name seemed to suit. It did look like a down-and-out old lady.

"I suggest you use some of those dollars I am paying you to buy a new car. That car is held together by rust and a couple of bolts."

"Don't insult my car, and I am not leaving it here to be stolen. I'm taking it home or I'm not going with you," Brinley stated, stubbornness in those light, unusual-but-exquisite silver green eyes.

Radd looked toward a black SUV parked a few spaces from them and jerked his head.

The doors immediately opened and his long-time chauffeur, Marcel, stepped out of the SUV.

"If you give Marcel your keys, they will make sure your car—" he refused to call it Betsy "—makes it home."

Radd thought there was a good chance that it would blow up or fall apart before it hit the motorway, but that wasn't his problem. And if it did, he could easily replace it with something better and safer.

A car that wasn't on its last legs. Or, he glanced down, on its last bald tire.

This woman had a death wish...and the thought made his heart cramp. Was he feeling concerned, a little protective and, if so, why? He'd met her *maybe* fifteen minutes ago.

She was not *his* problem, Radd reminded himself. She'd be out of his life by tomorrow afternoon, and he'd never think about her again.

Radd watched as Brinley reluctantly handed over her keys to Marcel, along with a long list of dos-and-don'ts. Frustrated, he stepped in and cut off her rambling explanation. "Marcel will figure it out. We need to go."

Panic flashed across her face, but then she straightened her shoulders, reached for her beach bag and pulled it through the open window. Radd turned to open the passenger door to his car to reveal a state-of-the-art interior. He liked his car; it was fast, technologically advanced and the best money could buy.

Brinley sighed, placed her bag on the floor and lowered herself into the comfortable leather bucket seat.

Radd kept his eyes on hers and watched as shock, then disbelief, jumped in and out of those incredible eyes. "Wait!"

What now? "Problem?"

"Did I hear you right? That you are paying me in US dollars? That's nearly four hundred thousand rand."

Radd lifted his brows at her shocked expression. "I can pay you twenty-five thousand in rand if you like."

Brinley sat back, folded her arms and shook her head. "You're mad. Who charges that sort of money for a day's work?"

"Apparently celebrity London-based florists," Radd responded, his tone super dry.

"Can we agree on the currency so we can get moving? Rand or US dollar?"

Brinley narrowed her eyes at him. "Oh, I'm not an idiot. If you're offering US, that's what I'm taking. And it's thirty, not twenty-five, because I made up my mind in a minute."

She was smart as well as beautiful. Beautiful was easy to dismiss, but brainy? Not so much. "Fine."

Radd closed her door, bid a smiling Marcel goodbye and, gesturing to her car, wished him good luck.

Marcel, with the familiarity of a staff member who'd taught him to ride a bike, then a motorcycle and a car, grinned at him. "I think you're going to need that good luck more than me."

And what, Radd wondered as he dropped into his seat, *the hell did Marcel mean by that*?

The bathroom on Radd's jet was almost as big as the one in her flat back home, but a thousand times more luxurious. Brin washed with the expensive toiletries she found in the cabinet, amused to find the air steward had left a glass of ice-cold Prosecco in the bathroom for her when he had went in to lay out some towels.

Brin, with one of those soft, huge towels wrapped around her frame, stepped into the master bedroom and eyed the massive king-size bed, covered in a blue-and-white duvet with a bold geometric pattern. Another glass of icy Prosecco stood on a coaster by the credenza, and her suitcase was already on a stool in the corner, ready to be flipped open.

Brin eyed the suitcase as she sipped her drink, yummy bubbles popping on her tongue. It was the bigger of her two suitcases. Why had Abby packed so much for an overnight trip? Shrugging, Brinley opened the lid and looked down at the hastily scrawled note on top of her clothes.

I had no idea what to pack for an overnight trip to one of the most luxurious places in the world, so I packed everything*!*

Woohoo! B, by next week you're going to have enough money to open Brin's Blooms! Feel free to spoil me.

Seriously, I'm happy for you.
Have fun. Love you!
xxx

Brin sat down on the bed, suddenly over-whelmed. This morning she'd left for an afternoon at the beach, and now she was on a jet, flying northeast, accompanied by the sexiest man she'd ever met.

And, provided she didn't mess up, she'd have more than enough money to open up her own florist shop, to pay the deposit and several months' rent, to buy stock.

Hell, she'd even probably have enough left over to buy a new car. Sorry, Betsy, but locks would be great, and air-conditioning even better.

Could she do this? Brin's fingers clutched the cool cotton of the bedcovers, hanging on for dear life. Oh, the dream of owning her own business was, in theory, lovely. It was easy to dream big when the possibility of success was remote but if nearly a half-million rand hit her bank account, she'd have to act, to put her money where her mouth, or her mind, was.

Brin gulped. Would she succeed with little to no experience? So many small businesses failed within the first year, would hers be any different? And was she cut out to be the boss, to make the decisions? She'd always worked in the background, taking orders rather than giving them, implementing someone else's visions and decisions.

Could she make her own?

But what choice did she have? She'd rather stab herself between her eyebrows with a rusty fork than go home, admitting to her mom and sister that she couldn't cut it.

If she did this, she'd have to *trust* and *believe* in herself.

Take a deep breath, Brinley. All she had to do was arrange some flowers and put up with Mr Arrogant for a day. She'd worked for Kerry, the definition of difficult, for years, so she knew she could deal with a bossy, arrogant, emotionally unavailable man with shadows in his eyes.

Brin sipped her drink, the cool Prosecco sliding down her throat as she considered the man sitting in the lounge area of this flying palace. He was driven and determined and, yes, autocratic, but he intrigued her. Oh, within two minutes of meeting him she knew he was emotionally distant and naturally cynical. But Brin sensed that he was, under his can't-be-rocked exterior, turbulent. She saw it in the way his one index finger tapped a hard bicep, in the changing shades of blue of his eyes, in the way he hauled in air as if to calm himself.

It was as if finding a floral designer was a bother, beneath him, and…well, she supposed it was. He was a billionaire businessman, ruthless and, it was said, intolerant, so why was he the one running around organizing a floral designer for a pre-wedding week at his ranch? That was normally a task that would be delegated to an underling.

Brinley wasn't complaining, she was glad he'd offered her the job, but why was he bothering with what should be a minor detail in his life?

After racking her brain, there was only one reason she could think of that explained why he was involved in the minutiae of this wedding.

He was the groom and this was his low-key, possibly secret wedding. It was the only explanation that made sense.

And, frankly, Radd's impending marriage was a relief. She didn't believe in coloring outside the lines, hers or anyone else's, and his engagement meant she could, she *would*, stop thinking about whether his bottom lip was as soft as it looked, whether he had a six- or eight-pack, and whether he sported hip muscles sexy enough to make a girl weep.

Brin placed her chin on her hands and tried to make sense of her raging attraction to Radd Tempest-Vane. He was gorgeous, ripped, sexy...

Any normal woman with a pulse would be attracted to him. But he belonged to someone else and Brin Riddell didn't poach.

Besides, Brin wasn't looking to become involved with anyone, anywhere. She was just starting to reconnect with herself, to work out who she was away from her dominating sister and mother, and any type of relationship would jeopardize any progress she'd made.

Kerry's light had always shone so much brighter than hers, and competing was impossible. Brin always felt like she stood on the

outside of her family circle, knew her long-
ing to be accepted had always been her driving force.

But it was like trying to shove a square peg
in a round hole and she'd twisted herself up
into complicated knots asking for something
they'd never be able to give her, so she had to
look to herself for what she needed.

Now, after months of being away from
them, she was feeling less anxious, a lot
braver—she would never have jumped on an
offer like Radd's six months ago!—and a tad
more resilient.

Best of all, her heart, battered and bruised,
was starting to heal. And she'd never risk
it again. Any type of involvement—physical or emotional or a combination of both—
with a man like Radd, who was tough, hard
and alpha to the tips of his toes, would be the
equivalent of asking someone to use her heart
as a bowling ball.

Not happening.

Brin rolled her shoulders and twisted her
head from side to side. She'd veered off into
thinking about her past and that annoyed her,

Brin didn't live there anymore. She needed to concentrate on the fact that Radd Tempest-Vane was offering her the opportunity to be completely free of her family. She'd be a fool to allow him to see her attraction or allow it to derail this amazing opportunity.

She just needed to calm down and think rationally, drink some water and rehydrate. Maybe she needed some food.

Her stomach rumbled in agreement and Brin smiled. No, she *definitely* needed some food.

And—she eyed her suitcase—she needed to dress. Then she would walk back to Radd and ask him what he and his bride wanted her to do with the flowers waiting for her at Kagiso Lodge.

And maybe, if she asked nicely, the lovely steward with the gorgeous brown eyes would bring her something to eat.

Radd looked up at the sound of the door to the master suite opening and watched Brinley walk into the lounge area of the jet, dressed in an ivory-and-pink sleeveless dress printed with huge flowers. Her makeup was light but expertly applied and she'd pulled her hair back into a tail, making her cheekbones look more defined than they already were.

Radd squirmed as the jet lurched and bounced. He gripped the arm of his chair, irritated his captain hadn't warned him about turbulence. Then, he realized Brinley hadn't reacted to the dip and sway of the plane. He glanced out of the window and saw the clear blue sky and reluctantly admitted it was the woman in front of him making his stomach dive. It had nothing to do with the weather, the plane or the pilot.

Radd leaned sideways to take another look out the window, struck by the dry beauty of the Karoo landscape miles below. He'd done this trip a hundred times, more, but he'd never noticed the beautiful, arid landscape was touched by patches of green and purple. His country, Radd admitted, had its problems, but God, it was so beautiful.

He couldn't wait to get to Kagiso, though this trip would be less relaxing than usual thanks to his sexy companion and the wedding party due to descend on Monday.

But at least he had a day and two nights to enjoy Kagiso, the favorite of all his properties. He loved the bush and the animals, but he was honest enough to admit that he also adored Kagiso because there were no memories of his parents associated with the ranch.

No fights, no strange people in wrong beds, no loud music, fights and screaming accusations. The cops had never arrived at Kagiso, no divorces had been demanded or hospital visits required.

Unlike their family home, the two-hundred-year-old farmhouse set among ancient vines, Kagiso was never mentioned in the newspapers or the tabloids.

Digby didn't care so much but he loathed being talked about, hated gossip. The only news coverage he was prepared to tolerate was related to business or his role as co-CEO of Tempest-Vane holdings.

Radd shifted in his chair, uncomfortable. He tried not to think of the past but, occasionally, he did find himself wishing for the moon: that Jack was still alive, that his parents had loved their sons more than they loved money, the attention of the press, and their constant pursuit of pleasure, that his father hadn't plundered, stripped and sold their heritage...

But the past couldn't be changed, so looking back was futile. It was far better to think of nothing at all, it was easier not to remember, to stay numb. And the best way to do that was to concentrate on work.

And that was why he was on a plane flying north, for *work*.

And Brinley was just another person who'd dropped into his life for twenty-four hours. The day after next she'd be a memory, a week from now she'd be forgotten. He had a mine to buy, a PR and rebranding exercise to plan, and a company to expand.

He wouldn't countenance any distractions.

No matter how sexy they were.

Radd, sitting on the far end of the four-seater couch, gestured for Brinley to take the chair to the right of him, thinking it was better to keep the source of temptation at a safe distance. Brinley sat down, crossed her long, lovely legs and Skye, his steward, hurried forward to ask her if she required more Prosecco.

Brinley refused alcohol and asked for sparkling water. Then she gestured to the fruit bowl on the table in front of them. "Do you mind? I missed lunch and I'm starving."

Skye, well trained, immediately responded with an offer to make her anything she wanted. And that wasn't a boast, Radd had once made an offhand comment in Skye's presence about craving sushi and, in no time at all, he had a perfectly plated platter placed in front of him.

Brinley smiled at Skye. "Oh, would you mind? A grilled cheese sandwich would be wonderful but, if it's a hassle, I'll just eat fruit."

Skye looked disappointed at receiving such a prosaic request. "I'm sure we can do better than a toasted sandwich," he replied. "Is there anything you don't eat or are allergic to?"

Brinley shook her head. She grinned at Skye, those sexy, deep dimples flashing and...yep, Radd's stomach launched itself off its sky-high diving board again.

Seriously, this was beyond ludicrous. He could easily imagine Digby rolling on the floor at his dilemma, laughing his ass off.

Because Radd was never knocked off-balance.

By anything.

His parents—and life—had thrown all manner of trials his way and he'd negotiated his way around all of them, most—Jack's death being the exception—without allowing the world to see him breaking a sweat. He'd trained himself not to react, to meet both victory and failure dispassionately, and rarely responded with anything other than impassivity. It helped that he went out of his way to avoid trouble and gossip.

He never gave the press anything to talk about because he couldn't stand to have his private life played out in the public domain.

"No, I'm poor so I can't afford to be fussy," Brinley told Skye, pulling his attention back to the present.

Skye wrinkled his nose, sympathy in his eyes. "I hear you, sister."

Radd snorted. Skye, like all of his staff, was exceptionally well paid. He and Digby were demanding, he wouldn't argue with that, but their staff were well recompensed.

Skye rubbed his hands together. "I'll see what I can conjure up. Radd, is there anything, in particular, you'd like?"

Radd saw Brinley's surprise at Skye's lack of formality. Radd was the boss and everyone knew it, so calling him "sir" didn't mean anything. Besides, Skye was older than him and Radd didn't need, or like, toadying.

He just needed people to do their job, and Skye did his particularly well. "Whatever you make will be fine with me. You can bring me some sparkling water, too."

Skye nodded, told them he'd be back in a few and left the stateroom, leaving them alone. Radd leaned back in his seat and linked his fingers together on his flat stomach, content to watch Brinley's profile as she stared out of the window into the endless blue below.

"How long until we land?" she asked without making eye contact.

Radd checked the time. "Probably about an hour. It'll be dusk when we arrive."

Brinley turned back to face him. She leaned

back in her seat and Radd saw the flash of ivory-colored wedge-heeled shoes with ribbons wound around shapely ankles. She was such a contradiction, and he couldn't quite make her out.

Her dress was designer, but the shoes weren't. The bikini she'd had on earlier was expensive, but her flip-flops were the type that could be bought at any flea market. She drove a worn-out car, but her beach bag was Gucci.

She was a paradox. He didn't like being curious. He wished he didn't feel the urge to pepper her with questions and he didn't care for not having the answers.

"Why are you frowning at my shoes?"

Radd jerked his head up to look into her eyes, wishing he could call them silver or green, yet they were neither one shade nor the other. They were a curious, lovely combination of both.

Radd wondered whether they'd darken or lighten or change color in anger or, more interestingly, when she was consumed by desire...

Dammit, Tempest-Vane! Not helpful.

"Uh…" Radd wiped his hand over his face before gesturing to her dress. "Cheap shoes, fancy dress. Expensive bag, crappy car."

Embarrassment skipped through her eyes before she lifted her stubborn, proud chin. "My sister is in the—" Brinley hesitated before continuing "—fashion industry and has a closet bigger than most clothing stores. Up until I moved to Cape Town six months ago, she passed a lot of her clothes on to me."

She was obviously reluctant to talk about her sister and that made him curious. Why did she move to Cape Town? Was he imagining the tinge of annoyance he heard in her voice?

She was his temporary employee, a woman who'd be out of his life tomorrow afternoon. He didn't need to dig into her life, for God's sake. He needed to get this conversation, and his thought patterns, back on track. She was only here to do a job for him.

It suddenly occurred to Radd that, in his haste to acquire a florist, he didn't know if she had any skills. This was not, by any stretch of the imagination, his finest day.

"How much experience do you have in flower arranging?" he demanded.

Brin looked at him from under long, thick lashes. "Mmm, not much. I'm more of a buy-flowers-from-the-garage-and-shove-them-into-a-glass-vase type."

Oh, God, he was so screwed.

Brin grinned, leaned forward and patted his knee. "Relax, I'm joking."

His heart restarted with a lurch and a shudder. "Not funny," he growled, surprised she had the cheek to tease him. Few people were that brave.

"I couldn't resist," Brin said, amusement dancing in her eyes. She reached into her bag, pulled out her phone and tapped the screen.

She held the device out to him and told him to swipe left to see her photos. He flipped through, saw wedding bouquets and huge tumbling arrangements, and tried to act like he knew what he was looking at. They looked fine, which was a relief.

"I've done a few weddings, some corporate functions and arrangements for parties. I've always loved flowers and gardening and making stuff grow." Brin told him, and he heard a note of insecurity in her voice. "It used to be a hobby, but I'm good enough to turn it into a career. Or so my clients tell me."

He wasn't in the business of handing out reassurances or support, and he'd never been the cheerleading type—he most definitely wasn't a hand-holder—but the urge to allay her insecurities was strong. Radd gripped the bridge of his nose and applied pressure to push these uncomfortable notions out of his head. Brin was not like anyone he'd ever met and she, for some reason, possessed the power to disarm him.

Why this woman and why now? He needed to stay detached, to be indifferent and emotionally uninvolved. He'd trained himself to be stoic and disengaged, but there was something about Brinley that made him want to step out of his carefully crafted cocoon.

He had to stop, retreat and pull himself together. If he had any sense, he'd pull out his laptop and ignore her for the rest of the flight.

He was paying her to do a job, he wasn't required to entertain her.

Brin leaned forward and pointed to her phone. "So is my work okay?"

Radd handed her phone back and shrugged. "I guess. I don't know anything about what you do." There was no way he'd tell her he liked the unstructured arrangements the best, they looked wild and free and...lush.

Lush? Holy hell, who was this person who'd taken possession of his mind?

Brin looked momentarily disappointed at his reply but she recovered quickly, and he appreciated the fact she didn't pout or sulk. "Can you give me some idea of what flowers I'll have to work with?" Brinley asked, putting her phone back in her bag. "And what you want?"

Was this a trick question? "I think they are blue. And we need them in vases."

Brinley gave him a look that was part amusement and complete frustration. "And that's all you have for me?"

"Pretty much," Radd admitted.

"Excellent," Brinley murmured, sarcasm coating every syllable. Skye placed two glasses filled with ice in front of each of them and cracked open a bottle of water.

"Well, will your fiancée be at the lodge?

Maybe she can spare some time to give me an idea of what she wants," Brinley asked.

His...*what?*

Radd heard Skye's snort and sent him a hot glare. Skye's expression turned neutral and he quickly finished pouring their drinks. When he left the room, Radd looked at Brinley. "Why would you think I'm the one getting married?"

"You aren't?"

Radd noticed her dismay and wondered why she looked so damn disappointed on hearing he wasn't about to be hitched and stitched. To clarify, he told her he was very single. Then he wondered why he felt the need to do so, because explaining wasn't something he ever did.

Radd watched as Brinley hunted for a reason for her confusion. "I just thought that, because you are so involved in all of this, you have a personal connection to the event. Men of your...um, men like you, high-flying businessmen, have people to organize stuff like this."

Fair point. But those were men who didn't have a multi-billion-dollar investment riding on this wedding and weren't dealing with a spoiled bride and her doting father.

Radd drank half of the contents of his glass before putting it back on the table. "It's crucial we keep the bride, and her father, happy, and trust me, they make it difficult."

Brinley's grasp on her glass loosened and the tension in her jaw eased. "Oh. Well, who is getting married and why do you need to keep them happy?"

He could tell her; it wasn't common knowledge, but neither was it a secret. "We are in negotiations with Vincent Radebe, he is selling us something we want. A condition of the sale is we provide his daughter Naledi with the best wedding experience possible. And that means pre-wedding festivities at Kagiso Ranch and an out-of-this-world wedding at The Vane next Saturday."

Radd had heard the expression *color drained from her face* before, but he'd never seen it happen until this moment. Brinley's eyes widened and, as her face paled, the freckles on her nose and cheeks stood out in stark relief.

She was going to faint, he just knew it.

Radd sprang to his feet and placed his hand against the back of her head, pushing her head gently down to rest between her knees, his fingers covered by soft, fragrant curls.

Maybe she'd had too much sun, too little food, or maybe she was dehydrated. It was possible.

Or maybe, just maybe, the fact she was doing flowers for a celebrity couple was overwhelming. Which was, he admitted, a little disappointing. Brinley didn't seem the swooning type.

She certainly hadn't with him.

CHAPTER THREE

HAVING STUMBLED BACK to the bathroom, Brinley gripped the basin and stared at her pale face in the mirror. Her eyes looked haunted and she'd chewed all her lipstick off. She looked like she felt, shocked but also resentful.

For the last few months, since she'd left Johannesburg and drastically reduced contact with her family, her life had been peaceful. She'd started sleeping well and stressing less, and she'd worked hard to find a new normal. While she wasn't completely happy—how could she be when she was constantly counting pennies?—she was content and that was, for now, enough.

The past six months had been drama free, but this day certainly wasn't. She didn't know where to start to try and make sense of it all...

Firstly, Radd Tempest-Vane wasn't engaged,

dammit, and he'd stripped her of the much-needed psychological barrier between them. If he was in love with someone else, she would've had a very good reason to ignore her attraction to him.

But the man had the temerity—the sheer audacity—to be single!

It didn't matter, Brin told herself, *it shouldn't matter.* Her insane physical reaction to him was nothing more than simple biology, an age-old instinct to mate, to procreate. She was young, healthy and yes, she had urges. This was a very normal reaction to a good-looking guy.

There was no need to overreact.

Besides, she had a far bigger problem than her inconvenient attraction to Radd.

Brinley straightened her arms and stared down at the expensive floor, sucking in deep breaths to get her heart to stop racing. There were a million couples at any one time who were in the process of getting married, but she was traveling to Kagiso Ranch to do the flowers for Naledi Radebe, Kerry's archenemy.

Naledi and her sister had once been friends,

good friends, but their relationship wasn't strong enough to survive Kerry being chosen instead of Naledi for some advertisement campaign. Then came the allegations of Kerry dating someone Naledi was seeing. At a party, slaps had been exchanged and the pictures in the press hadn't been pretty. Someone pressed assault charges, the other responded with charges of her own, though the criminal charges were eventually dropped and the fight moved to the civil courts.

Then came the social media war that left them both bleeding but, eventually, the vitriol eased and now it was just the occasional caustic tweet throwing shade. Neither had ever made the attempt to mend fences.

Knowing she needed more information, Brin picked up her phone, accessed the onboard Wi-Fi and did a quick search, immediately picking up an article announcing Naledi's engagement to Johnathan Wolfe and, God, yes, he was the same guy Kerry had had a fling with two years ago.

Oh, crap and dammit.

Reasonable or not, Naledi would lose it if she realized her enemy's sister was doing her flowers. It wouldn't matter to Naledi that Brin and Kerry seldom spoke, Brin shared Kerry's blood and that would be enough to make her lose it.

Kerry would probably also call her a traitor, screaming that blood should always stand with blood.

Nobody had ever called either of the two society princesses reasonable.

God, this was disastrous. Brin paced the small area of the bathroom, wondering what she should do. She could tell Radd her nebulous connection to the bride but if she did, he'd turn the plane around and dump her still-broke butt back in Cape Town. He had a massive business deal riding on the outcome of this wedding and he wouldn't risk upsetting the Radebes.

He'd find another florist, and she would be out of thirty thousand US dollars. She needed that money. Really, *really* needed it, and if she spent twenty-four hours at Kagiso and did a decent job, she could create a life that excited her…a little shop, and working as a floral designer, adding pops of color and interest to homes and events, would make her happy.

Unlike Kerry, she didn't need a big stage, or lights or action. It wasn't big or bold, but Brin didn't need big or bold, she just needed it to be *hers*.

Brin flicked her thumbnail against her bottom teeth. Radd had told her that she was due to leave the lodge tomorrow afternoon and the wedding party was only flying in on Monday morning. She could do the flowers, get paid enough to set up her own business and leave before Naledi arrived. She'd leave it up to Radd to explain who the florist was. She owed this to herself and, if she didn't take this opportunity, she'd regret it for the rest of her life.

Brinley looked at herself in the mirror, pleased to see the color had returned to her face and her eyes no longer looked haunted. Progress.

She could pull this off, she *had* to.

Brinley walked back into the salon to see Skye placing a platter between two bone china plates on the dining table. Silver cutlery, crystal glasses and three thousand count linen napkins made her think she was eating in a five-star restaurant.

Brinley stepped forward and saw the platter was, actually, a beautiful seafood salad—and she grinned. Thanks to her skeletal budget, seafood was something she never ate.

"Oh, Skye, it looks fantastic," Brin said, walking up to the table. Skye pulled out her chair and Brin sat down.

Radd walked over to the table and took his seat, pulling the bottle of white wine from the silver ice bucket. "You're looking better," he commented.

"Low blood sugar, I think," Brinley replied, as Skye piled seafood salad onto her plate.

Radd's eyes sharpened. "Are you sure that's all it was?"

Brin didn't like lying, but what choice did she have? She was not giving up her dreams, not when she just needed a scant twenty-four hours to make them come true.

She shrugged as she placed a linen serviette across her lap. "It's been an interesting day."

"Just so you know, Ms. Riddell, I don't like secrets or surprises. In fact, they are my least favorite thing in the world. So, if there's something I should know, tell me now."

Oh, wow, there was the ultra-tough, fantastically shrewd businessman. He was both sexy and a little scary, and Brin was thankful she'd never have to meet him in a boardroom. He'd chew her up and spit her out…

"I haven't eaten all day and am probably a little dehydrated. I'll be fine by the time we land," Brin hedged.

Radd looked skeptical, but Brin just kept her eyes on him, hoping he'd change the subject. It took everything Brin had not to look away, knowing that if she did, he'd see it as a sign of weakness or, worse, for the lie it was. Their stalemate was broken by Skye clearing his throat and they both turned their attention back to him.

"We'll be landing in forty minutes. Bon Appétit."

"Leave your bags," Radd told her. "The staff will take them up to the lodge."

Brinley nodded and followed him to the jet's exit. Even from a few steps away from the door, she could feel the air was different: warm but earthy, primal. As she stood at the top of the stairs and looked over the bush beyond the airstrip, she felt instantly connected to this old-as-time land.

Wide-open skies, fresh air, thick vegetation. It was wild and luscious and so different from the city life she was used to.

Brin noticed the open-top game viewing vehicles parked to the side of the airstrip, two rangers dressed in khaki shorts, dark green shirts and hiking boots next to them. Walking down the steps, Brin stopped, turned and looked back up to Radd, a few steps behind here.

"This is a ridiculous question but where, exactly, are we?"

Radd's stern mouth tipped up at the corners. "We're on the southern edge of the Kalahari Desert."

When they reached the grass strip, Radd took her hand—making bubbles pop on her skin—and tugged her away from the plane, turning her around to look in the opposite direction. Purple-blue, craggy mountains cast shadows over the plains below.

Conscious of her very small hand in his, Brin found her head dipping sideways to rest on his shoulder. She felt him tense, heard his intake of breath and slammed her eyes shut, mortified by her lover-like response. Abruptly, she pulled her hand from his, defiantly folding her arms across her chest.

Note to self: touching Radd makes your brain turn to mush.

Radd started to speak and Brin forced herself to concentrate.

"We're in what we call the green Kalahari," Radd explained. "The reserve is home to Kalahari black-maned lions, black desert rhino, Hartmann's mountain zebra, cheetah, gemsbok, roan antelope, the pangolin and many, many more animals. The guests, and the money they pay, fund our conservation efforts. The land and animals are our priority."

Brinley heard the tiny crack in his voice suggesting emotion and saw the passion in his eyes. In this brief moment, Radd wasn't the hard-ass billionaire businessman, but an ardent man advocating for something he believed in. Brin understood, at a fundamental level, how important Kagiso was to him.

Radd's cologne mixed with the smell of foliage, dust and wild Africa, and the combination made Brin's head swim. The fading rays of the sun touched his dark hair and turned his ink pot eyes to a shade of black. All Brin wanted to do was stand in this spot and taste Africa in his mouth and on his skin, feel his arms gathering her into his body.

Radd lifted his hand and he brushed his thumb over her bottom lip, then across her cheekbone. What was he doing? Where was this coming from? She thought she'd seen attraction and desire in his eyes but, because his expression remained implacable and because he was so out of her league, she wasn't sure.

Was she his type? Could he, possibly, be as attracted to her as she was to him?

Radd lowered his head and Brin thought, hoped, he might kiss her, but a millisecond later, he jerked his head back and stepped away from her.

"We are not going there, Brinley."

She took a quick, awkward step backward. Yes, of course, she knew that! Hadn't she been telling herself exactly that? Brinley stared into the distance, annoyed with herself. Why was the concept of Radd Tempest-Vane being strictly, completely, Area 51-off-limits not sinking in? She was reasonably intelligent, it wasn't a difficult concept to grasp.

Radd lightly touched her back and led her over to the first of the game viewing vehicles. One of the rangers immediately sprang into action, opening the front passenger door for her. When he put out a hand to help her into the vehicle, Radd spoke to him in an African language, his voice, as always, commanding.

The game ranger stepped back, replied and nodded.

"You speak… What language do they speak here?" Brin asked as she lifted her skirt to climb into the deep green vehicle. She placed her hand in his and allowed him to steady her as she stepped onto the running board. She settled in her seat as Radd walked around the vehicle and climbed into the driver's seat.

"Tswana," Radd rested his forearms on the wheel and stared at the thick bush on the other side of the airstrip. "*Kagiso* means peace in Tswana. I spent a lot of time here with my paternal grandfather as a kid, pretty much every school holiday. I'm told I could speak the language before I could speak English."

Wow. "That's amazing. I wish I spoke an African language."

Radd turned the ignition and the engine caught. "Why don't you? It's pretty obvious you have some African blood."

"My mother is biracial, and my biological father is white. My grandfather was Sotho, but we only ever spoke English at home," Brinley replied, not meeting his eyes. "My mother's side of the family left their culture behind a long time ago."

"That's sad."

He had no idea.

"Why are you driving and not your staff?" Brin asked, wanting to change the subject.

Radd changed gears as he navigated a sharp, upward turn to the left. He took his time answering and, for a moment, Brin didn't think he would. Eventually, he sighed and shrugged. "As a rule, I like to drive myself. And I've been driving these roads since I was ten years old. I love it here."

Brin frowned, not understanding. "More than you love your magnificent flat in Camps Bay or your vineyard in Stellenbosch?"

"Have you been researching me, Miss Riddell?" he asked in a silky voice.

"You wish." Brin snorted. "I know about your properties because your rooftop garden at your flat and the garden at your vineyard were both featured in a gardening magazine I subscribe to."

"Oh, right. I remember my landscaper asking me for permission to take the magazine photographer to both properties."

Brin thought Radd would be hard-pressed to describe either property, and was starting to suspect that Radd had tunnel vision and didn't see or care for much outside of work. If she had gardens like his, she'd never leave them.

Radd's hand tightened on the wheel and he opened his mouth to tell Brin those other properties were just assets he owned, but that he considered Kagiso his home, a place of freedom and peace.

His memories of this land were only happy ones...

The smell of grandfather's pipe, camping underneath the stars or in caves containing rock art done by the San people, running wild with Jack and Digby and the children of the staff working the ranch. Swimming in the concrete water reservoir on hot days, falling asleep to the sound of jackals barking at night. The three brothers making plans for the rest of their lives, plans that didn't include their parents...

Radd shook off his thoughts and when he turned his head to look at Brin, he saw the hulking shadow moving slowly in the distance. He braked, stopped and touched Brin's shoulder, pointing to a space between the trees.

"There's a black rhino at eleven o'clock. Highly endangered, completely awe-inspiring," Radd whispered.

Brin's hand landed on his thigh and Radd sucked in a deep breath as her fingertips burned through the fabric of his pants into his skin. Desire roared through him, as turbulent and as fierce as an African thunderstorm. He stared at her exquisite profile, reluctantly admitting he'd wanted her from the first moment he saw her standing near her worn-out Beetle earlier.

He. Wanted. Her.

More than he ever expected, more than he could believe. But this was just—*this had to be!*—a normal reaction of a man to a sexy woman; it didn't mean anything beyond a need to work off excess sexual energy.

He hadn't had sex for a while and he was past due. Right, when he used his brain, his attraction to Brinley was simple and easily explained.

The rhino moved deeper into the bush and Brinley sighed, a sweet, soft sound. His blood plummeted south as he wondered whether she sounded like that when she fell apart in a man's arms. Specifically, *his* arms.

Then she turned to look at him, her mouth now just a couple of inches from his own. In the sinking light, her eyes were the color of a mermaid's, now a silver-aqua shade and fully able to rip his breath away. Through her light makeup, he could see the hints of her freckles, and he wanted to pull her dress off her body and discover where else those sweet dots appeared. Her eyes locked on his and, in them, he saw awareness, desire and yearning: everything he was feeling.

He wanted to taste her, no, he needed to taste her. Just once so he could stop obsessing about whether her mouth was as sweet as he imagined.

Radd touched his lips to hers, aiming to keep his kiss light, chaste if he could. But a few seconds after their lips connected, she opened her lips and he couldn't resist, he had to go on in. His tongue pushed past her teeth to slide against hers and she arched her back in that feminine, age-old silent way of asking for more.

But instead of waiting for him to give her what she wanted, Brin, surprising the hell out of him and without breaking contact with his mouth, turned in her seat. Moving gracefully, she lifted her skirt and straddled him, bent knees on either side of his thighs. She reached for his shirt and bunched the fabric in her hands as she deepened the kiss, asking, no, demanding, more.

Thoughts of resistance flew out of his brain. His hands found the bottom of her dress and he pulled it up so his hands could stroke the back of her smooth thighs, roam over her gorgeous backside covered in cool cotton. He explored the valley of her lower back, the curve of her slim hip, her luscious butt. Pulling away from her mouth, he kissed his way up her jaw, down her neck, but Brin moved her hand from his chest back to his face, tipping his head so she could feast on his mouth again.

And feast she did. So much passion rested under her surfer-girl exterior and he wanted more, he wanted all of her. He wanted her tongue in his mouth, but also wanted it on his neck. He wanted her hands on his chest, in his pants. He wanted to explore all her valleys and dips, the knobs of her spine, the ball of her shoulder, discover the color of her nipples, taste the sweetness between her legs.

He didn't think he'd ever wanted anyone as much, or as fast, as he wanted Brinley Riddell. And for the first time in, well, forever, his reaction terrified him. Women never knocked him sideways, he refused to give them that much power. That Brin could was...

Bizarre. Unsettling.

And yes, completely unacceptable.

The low rumble of a vehicle pierced the

night sounds of the bush and Radd quickly reacted. In one smooth movement, he lifted Brinley off his lap and deposited her back in her seat and. a few seconds later, he cranked the engine and pulled away as the lights of the other vehicle appeared behind him.

Brin whipped around to look at the second vehicle before slumping back in her seat. "Wow. Close call."

"I'm their boss and the owner. If they caught us naked, they'd turn a blind eye," Radd replied, his tone brusque.

Brin didn't reply, but Radd felt her eyes on his profile and wondered if her heart, like his, was about to jump out of her chest, whether she wanted him to stop the vehicle and resume where they left off.

He very much did.

Radd stared at the dirt ahead, easily navigating around a chameleon in the middle of the road. Out of the corner of his eye, he could see her chest rising and falling quickly, the small tremor in her fingers resting on her slim thigh.

Yeah, she was equally affected.

The chemistry between them could not be

denied; it was a living, breathing entity. Could it be bigger and bolder than what he normally experienced because he'd gone without sex for too long? Radd did some mental arithmetic and realized the last time he'd gotten laid was four, and a bit, months ago… No wonder he felt like a pressure cooker about to blow.

But honesty compelled him to reluctantly admit that, while he felt frustrated by his lack of bed-based activity, it wasn't the longest period he'd gone without sex and he'd never felt this off-balance before. Forty percent might be sexual frustration, the rest was his unexpected and unwelcome need to kiss Brinley from tip to toe, to discover her secrets, to hear what noises she made when she came, whether she was as tight and warm and fabulous as he imagined her to be.

Brinley was sexy and smart but, under her natural passion, he could tell that she was inexperienced, a little unsure. While he preferred women who were more skilled, who could keep up with him in the bedroom, he rather liked the idea of teaching Brin a little of what he knew…

Radd slapped his hand against the back of

his neck and welcomed the slight sting in his hand. She was his employee, she'd be out of his life tomorrow night, and he wasn't the type to seduce innocents. And, despite being in her late twenties, if she wasn't innocent, then she was definitely inexperienced.

And, no matter how sweet her kisses or how deep her passion ran, he wasn't anyone's teacher. Except for being Digby's brother, he wasn't anyone's anything.

Besides, he'd watched the crap show that was his parents' marriage and had front row seats to how love made people irrational, how it made them lose control. Every relationship, good, bad and dysfunctional, required work and involvement and emotion, and he didn't have the time or inclination. He kept his relationships at surface level. If you didn't allow anyone behind the armor, no one could do any damage. If one didn't engage, actions and words couldn't be misconstrued.

It was a simple concept that served him well. And Brinley Riddell—free-spirited, gorgeous, inexperienced and intriguing— would not be the first to find his chinks.

And to ensure that didn't happen—it

wouldn't, but Radd never took chances—
he'd keep his distance. He'd drop her off at
the lodge and retreat to his private villa at the
end of the property. He had his laptop and
enough work to keep him occupied and, if
the gods were smiling on him, Brinley would
complete her flower arranging in record time
and he could whip her back to Cape Town,
pay her and put her out of his mind.

That was the plan, because the other plan
fighting for his attention—to keep her, naked,
in his bed for the next twenty-four hours—
was not only a nonstarter, but stupid.

He was reserved, implacable, emotionally
detached and occasionally difficult, but stupid he was not.

CHAPTER FOUR

SHE'D KISSED RADD TEMPEST-VANE, the man who held her future in his admittedly exceptionally skilled hands.

Idiot. Idiot. Idiot.

Brin licked her lips, thinking she could still taste him—fresh, gorgeous, comprehensively, powerfully male—on her lips, on her tongue. She hadn't had much time to explore his body, but she knew his thighs were strong, his stomach ridged with muscle, his chest wide. His hands were big, broad and capable, and his arms powerful.

One touch of his lips to hers and she'd turned into a wild woman, devoid of sense and thought. Oh, she'd like to be able to say that she would've retreated had he pushed for more, but she didn't know if that was the truth.

His hands on her legs and butt had felt so amazing and, had she been able to form the words or pull her mouth from his, she'd would've begged him to touch her breasts, to slide a big hand between her thighs.

She wanted him. More than she'd ever wanted anyone or anything before.

She was *so* screwed.

One kiss, a mild grope and it was like she hadn't spent most of the past half day telling herself why hooking up with Radd was a comprehensively bad, bad, *terrible* idea. Maybe she should just record a voice note and push play every time she forgot the hundred reasons why she shouldn't kiss/touch/sleep with Radd Tempest-Vane.

Shall we list them again? For the hundredth and sixtieth time?

She was in the process of finding her authentic self, working on her insecurities, her dark thoughts. She did not need to complicate the process with unwanted attraction.

And it *was* unwanted, because Radd was who and what she didn't need. Having just rid herself of two bossy people, she did not want another super confident, autocratic, overbearing person in her life.

No matter how gorgeous, sexy, hot and rich he was….

And man, he was stupidly rich.

Brin sighed. While she'd been exposed to her sister's rich-ish existence, it was nothing compared to Radd's billionaire lifestyle, and she didn't know how to operate in such a rarified world. Few, she imagined, would. Nor did she want to, money wasn't what drove her. Being accepted, feeling like she belonged, did. Radd's universe—rich, opulent and excessive—wasn't what she was looking for.

It wasn't where she belonged. It would gobble her up and spit her, and her battered and bruised heart, out. It was a scenario she'd prefer to avoid, thank you very much.

Oh, and she was kind of…sort of…keeping a secret from him. But, since it wouldn't impact their deal, she could live not telling him about Kerry's and Naledi's stupid feud.

Hands off him, Brinley Riddell, no matter how much you want to touch. Just do your job, get paid and slide out of his life. Brin glanced at her watch, squinting at the dial in the ultra-low light. *You have to be here for another twenty or so hours, surely you can control your heart and your mind and your hands for that long?*

And her mouth! For someone who'd always had a problem talking back, her mouth was working at supersonic speed. What was up with that?

Brin caught the glimpse of lights between the trees and, as Radd steered the vehicle up a steep hill, the lights became brighter and bolder. He turned to the left and there, on the edge of a cliff, sat an impressive building that looked like part of the landscape. Brin looked beyond the building to the plain, stretching out for many miles below. Her breath caught and, taking in the exceptional view, all thoughts of seeing Radd naked faded away.

Radd stopped the car and they took in the vista as the blood-red sun dipped below the horizon. She could see animals moving slowly across the plain but, because they were too far away, couldn't identify the creatures.

This was Africa: wild, vast and incomprehensively beautiful.

Far too soon, Radd accelerated away and parked the vehicle closer to the entrance of the lodge. He half turned in his seat to face her. "My manager, Mari, will meet you inside and, after getting you settled into your room, she'll show you what you have to do and where you can work. The lodge is empty at the moment, you will be the only guest tonight. The chef has prepared supper for you and Mari will be on hand to bring you anything you require—food, snacks, tools, wire, whatever you need."

"Oh, um… I thought you'd be staying here, too," Brin said. Not sure whether to be pleased or disappointed, Brin nibbled the inside of her cheek. Being alone would give her some time to shore up her defenses, to get her head on straight.

But being alone would mean not being with Radd. Her body very much wanted to be near Radd, stupid thing.

"There are guest rooms within the lodge and a handful of suites. My personal suite, we call them villas, is at the far end of the property." Radd ran his hands through his hair in an impatient gesture. "Let's clear the air, Brin,"

Brin wrinkled her nose. *Ack*, a conversation starting with those words rarely went well.

Radd rested his forearms on the steering wheel and stared past the hood of the vehicle to the dark shadows beyond. Brin followed his gaze and saw him looking at an expansive deck. Brin saw dark water and realized the entertainment area ended in a large infinity pool, its water seeming to tumble off the side of the cliff.

Oh, wow, she couldn't wait to see Kagiso Lodge in daylight. It would, she was sure, live up to all her expectations.

"For some strange, inexplicable reason, you seem to be forgetting you are here to work, Miss Riddell. I am paying you an extraordinary amount of money to arrange flowers. You are here to do a job."

Brin's eyes slammed into his and the deep navy, almost black, eyes were harder than she'd ever seen them. His lips were now thin slashes in his face and a deep frown pulled her attention to his hard-as-granite eyes.

He was acting as if she were the only one who'd enjoyed their kiss, like she'd thrown herself at him, like she was at fault. *Seriously?*

"Are you reminding yourself or me?" Brin demanded, once again surprised at her fast response and lack of deference. She really didn't recognize this mouthy person!

Radd just stared at her, his expression inscrutable. She'd known him for just a few hours, but she didn't like him hiding behind that enigmatic expression.

Don't rock the boat, Brin, just swallow the hot words in your throat. Just exit the vehicle and walk away.

But that was what she always did, and this time she wanted a reaction. She refused to slink into the shadows, happy to accept the blame for something that wasn't her fault. Maybe she'd grown a spine since leaving Johannesburg.

"Might I remind you that you kissed me, that your hands were on my butt, your fingers slid under the band of my panties? I was not alone in the madness. I know why I am here, *Mr. Tempest-Vane*. I haven't forgotten, not for a minute. But don't you dare pretend, oh-so-suddenly, that the attraction is all on my side."

Radd released an irritated sigh, his broad shoulders lifting and falling. "Fine, our kiss got out of hand, I'll admit you are right, I *am* attracted to you. But I'm damned if I'm going to do anything about it." Radd muttered. "You're not my type, you're too..."

Oh, this should be good. "I'm too... What?"

She heard the whoosh of his breath, what might have been a hot curse followed by the word "dangerous." He thought she was dangerous? That couldn't be right. What threat could she pose to Radd Tempest-Vane?

"Go on in, Brinley," Radd said. "Mari is inside, she'll sort you out."

He sounded exhausted, like he was all out of patience with her and the situation. Brinley, no longer prepared to hang around when she wasn't wanted, picked her bag up off the floor and reached for the handle of the door.

"I'll see you in the morning," Brin told him, determined to hold on to her manners. One of them should.

Holding her bag strap, Brin walked up the steps leading into what she presumed was the lobby of the hotel. There was no reception desk, just two expensive, stone-colored modern couches facing each other and, above them, two massive abstract paintings reflecting the colors of the rapidly fading sunset.

Turning left, Brin walked into an open plan lounge and instantly realized why all the travel magazines rated this one of the most luxurious lodges in the world. The furniture was obviously expensive but looked incredibly comfortable, deep cushions and gleaming wooden side tables and footstools in greens and golds and browns, all the colors of the African bush.

She could get lost in the decor, but her eyes were immediately drawn to the huge floor-to-ceiling sliding doors that were pushed open to reveal the deep deck and the sparkling infinity pool. As the sun faded, stars popped through the deepening darkness, first one, then another, then a handful.

The air smelled verdant and rich and primal, and Brin placed her hand on her heart, conscious, yet again, of that strange feeling of connection.

Despite never visiting this part of the country before, her soul recognized this place...

"Miss Riddell?"

Brin, not wanting to pull her eyes off the night sky, reluctantly turned around and watched a slim woman cross the deck to her, her elegant hand outstretched. This Iman lookalike had to be Mari, Radd's manager.

God, she was gorgeous.

"Welcome to Kagiso."

"Thank you, it's beautiful," Brin replied.

Mari lifted her eyebrows. "Radd didn't accompany you in?"

Brin shrugged. "He went on to his villa."

"As I'm sure you want to do, as well," Mari smoothly replied.

"I'm really happy to stay here and look at the stars," Brin confessed.

Mari sent her a small smile. "Well, in your villa, you can soak in an outdoor bath and look at the stars."

Oh, God, that sounded...blissful. Indulgent, luxurious.

"And I can send your dinner to your room, along with any beverage you desire."

It was Brin's turn to raise her eyebrows. *Anything* was a big word. "Anything at all?"

Mari nodded. "Pretty much."

Wow. Okay, then. Brin looked up at the diamond-on-velvet sky again before following Mari's long-legged stride inside the lodge. She crossed the slate floor, running her hand along the top of a butter-soft leather couch, her eyes taking in the world-class sculptures on the floor and stunning art on the wall.

Good job, Radd. This is amazing.

Mari opened a side door and led her down a stone pathway, past a cozy library and what looked to be a beautifully appointed office. "Yours?" Brin asked her.

Mari laughed. "I wish! No, that is the office the guests use for the important calls, video conferences and emails they can't afford to miss. That's the only room where there is Wi-Fi, otherwise we encourage our guests to disconnect to reconnect."

She'd avoid the office, Brin thought, smiling, liking the idea of being unreachable.

"And this is our multipurpose room, we can hold mini-conferences here or cocktail parties or discos." Mari stopped by a door at the end of the main building and pushed open the door. She flicked on a light and moved back to allow Brin to enter the room.

"Why would anyone want to be here when they could be on the deck?" Brin asked but didn't wait for a reply, her attention caught by the various shades of blue flowers standing in buckets on the long stainless-steel table.

There were delphiniums, blue hydrangeas, cream roses and lilies, blue grape hyacinths, blue roses and delicate orchids and freesias. Brin dropped her bag to the floor and hurried to the table, dipping her head to smell the freesias, running her finger over the delicate petals of a creamy, blue-tinted rose. Her eyes danced over her supplies, huge glass vases and earthenware pots, tape, shears and wire, delicate ribbon and buckets of glossy green fillers. A list of arrangements sat on the desk and Brin quickly perused it, making adjustments here, leaving or adding flowers there.

Looking at the stars from a bubble bath could wait, because she'd just stepped into her own version of heaven. And it was filled with flowers.

* * *

It was just past five the next morning when Radd walked into the dining room and headed straight for the coffee machine in the corner. He jammed his cup under the spout. At the sound of footsteps, he turned and smiled when he saw one of his oldest friends crossing the room to where he stood.

"You're up early," Mari said after they exchanged a hug. "Did you sleep well?"

That would be a no. He'd tossed and turned for hours, unable to push the memory of how Brinley tasted from his thoughts. He'd kissed a lot of women, slept with about as many, but he'd never lost sleep before. He didn't like it.

He seemed to be saying that a lot around Brin.

Speaking of Brinley, he wondered where she was. The door to her villa had been open when he'd passed by and her bed had been made. He'd called out but received no reply.

"Did you arrange for one of the rangers to take Brin on a game drive?" Radd asked as Mari fixed herself a cup of coffee.

"No, I wouldn't have done that without

your permission," Mari answered him, a tiny frown marring her smooth forehead.

Then where the hell was she? "She's not in her room, have you seen her this morning?"

Radd felt his stomach lurch and cold water ran through his veins. God, he hoped she hadn't gone for a walk. The resort wasn't fenced and the animals—wild, free and dangerous—could, and had, stroll through the grounds. Just last week they'd had a leopard lying in the branches of the acacia outside villa four.

He'd been so desperate to lay his hands, and his mouth, on her that he hadn't given her the safety speech. Goddammit, how could he be so stupid?

Mari placed a hand on his arm. "I'm sure she's fine, Radd. Let's just stay calm, okay?"

Right. He never panicked, so why was his throat tight and his lungs heaving? Pulling in a few deep breaths, he shook his head to clear it, and forced away thoughts of Brinley being mauled by a hyena or bitten by a Cape cobra.

Overreacting much, Tempest-Vane?

"Why don't you check the conference

room?" Mari suggested. "Maybe she decided to get up early to get the arrangements done."

Now, why hadn't he thought of that first? Oh, maybe because he'd had no sleep, was sexually frustrated and generally pissed off that a woman he'd met yesterday—yesterday, for God's sake!—had managed to rock his world.

He couldn't wait for later, to be able to bundle her onto his plane and send her back to Cape Town and out of his life. He didn't like feeling this off-kilter, so out of control.

Control wasn't just important, it was *everything*.

Holding his coffee cup, Radd walked out of the dining room and down the stone path leading to the conference room. He opened the door to the light-filled room, his eyes widening at the enormous bouquets sitting on the steel table in the middle of the room. They were a riot of white, cream, blues and greens, lush and wild. Somehow, despite the flowers being imported and exotic, she'd managed to invoke the feel of the bush in the arrangements. He was reminded of the colors of new spring growth, the African sky in summer, the way the sun hit the land at the beginning of the day.

The buckets on the floor were mostly empty, save for a couple of stalks of greenery.

Her work was done, and done exceptionally well, but where the hell was Brin?

Walking farther into the room, Radd's booted foot kicked something soft, and he looked down to see a leather tote bag lying on the floor. Radd looked around. Seeing the high-backed couch at the other end of the room, he strode over to it and his heart finally settled into an even rhythm. Brin was curled up on the plump cushions, her hands tucked under her head, dark curls resting on her cheek. Since she wore the same clothes as yesterday, it was obvious she'd never made it to her room last night.

He gently picked up one curl, then another, and pulled them off her cheek. Her makeup had worn off and he could see the spray of freckles on her straight nose, a tiny scar in the middle of her forehead. Her eyelashes, long and thick, touched her cheek and highlighted the blue stripes under her eyes. How late had she worked?

Radd gripped the back of the couch and stared down at her, fighting the wave of lust threatening to consume him. He could handle desire, he wasn't a kid and could walk away, but the wave of protectiveness surprised him. He wasn't sure what to do with it.

Why was he feeling this way? Why was he feeling anything at all? He wasn't used to paying this much attention to his feelings, to even *having* feelings. He'd trained himself not to react, to push emotion away.

He needed to go back to feeling nothing.

And he would, because Brinley wasn't, in any way, his type. He dated—okay, slept with—sophisticated women, tough women, women who knew the score.

He dated cool blondes and raven-haired pixies, African queens and fiery redheads. Looks weren't important, but their emotional independence was.

So why the hell had he kissed Brin last night? Why had he spent hours last night imagining what her slim, firm and glorious naked body would feel like pressed up against his—damn good, of that he had no doubt.

Why, goddammit, was he standing here staring down at her?

There was only one explanation: he was losing his damned mind. He should only have one priority, and that was making sure that Naledi's wedding went off without a hitch and getting Vincent to sign the final deed of sale. Restoring the mine to the Tempest-Vane group of companies was all that was important.

The acquisition of the mine, and their announcement that they would be increasing capacity and employing thousands of workers, would be front-page news. That news would lead to an interest in their PR and rebranding exercise.

They would garner attention, but it would be the *right* sort of attention.

The hope was that the PR campaign and the rebranding exercise would, finally, dilute the interest in his parents fast-paced and over-the-top lives, and their still recent deaths. More than a few journalists had, over the years, blown up minor incidents in his and Digby's lives, trying to show that he and his brother were like Gil and Zia. Digby's escapades—fast cars, boats and bikes and his one-date love life— garnered attention but nothing he did was ever, thank God, salacious. Or smarmy.

Scandal sold papers, but Radd was determined to show the world they were apples that had fallen very, very far from the family tree.

Along with a couple of personal interviews he intended to give to trusted journalists, the world would see that he and Digby were serious, responsible and restrained. That the Tempest-Vanes could be trusted again.

Damn you, Gil and Zia.

Radd rubbed his jaw and hauled in a deep breath, seeking calm. Thinking about his parents reminded him of his need to remain numb. Feelings, he'd decided a long time ago, were counterproductive. Love was a mirage, a myth and a lie.

Besides, Brinley wasn't his type.

He was repeating himself. Again. He obviously needed more sleep and so, he presumed, did she.

Responding to his squeeze of her shoulder, Brin slowly opened her eyes and Radd was briefly reminded of that photo of the

Afghan Mona Lisa, the girl with the light green eyes in her dark face. Brin's skin tone was much lighter, but her eye color was as intense, splashes of light in her face.

Gorgeous.

"What time is it?" Brin asked, her voice sexy with sleep.

"Just after six," Radd replied as she swung her long legs off the couch. She stretched and the hem of her T-shirt rose an inch, maybe two, revealing a strip of smooth skin. He wanted to put his mouth on that strip, nudging the shirt up with his nose to find her breast, her nipple.

Or go lower...

Radd cursed and tipped his head back to look at the high ceiling. It was going to be a long, long day, but by this afternoon she'd be on his plane. Then he'd be able to forget her and her irritating effect on him.

Yet the thought of her leaving left a bitter taste in his mouth. That had to be because Brin's company was preferable to Naledi's and her father's, to that of the guests he had yet to meet.

Brin stood up and bent down to touch her

toes, wrapping her arms behind her knees and pushing her pert bottom in the air. Oh, hell, she was bendy...

Not what he needed to know.

"Did you sleep here last night?"

Yeah, he understood he was being rude, but rude was better than taking her in his arms, lowering her to the couch and doing several things to her he was pretty sure this couch, or this room, had never seen. Or maybe, knowing his guests, it had.

"I finished around two," Brin said, unfurling her long body and standing up straight. She placed her hand over her mouth to cover her yawn. She looked past him to the bouquets of flowers on the table. "What do you think?"

There was that note of insecurity in her tone again, the silent wish to be reassured. Normally he would ignore it, but Brin had done a great job and what would it hurt to tell her so? "They look amazing," he truthfully answered.

Brin's eyes locked on his as a hopeful smile touched her lips. "Really? Honestly?"

"I never say things I don't mean."

Brin walked over to the table, pulled out a cream rose only to jam it back into the same spot. "I'm not happy with the balance of this one."

Radd put his hand over hers and pulled it away from the arrangement. Goosebumps raised the hair on his arms and blood flowed south, tenting his pants. And all because he was holding her hand. Could he be any more ridiculous? Radd dropped her hand and, to keep from reaching for her and showing her how much he appreciated her efforts in a more basic, biblical way, he shoved his hands into the pockets of his jeans.

Brin stepped away from the table and turned her back on the flowers. "Full disclosure, I didn't follow the exact instructions of the original florist. She wanted more structured arrangements, but I think these work a lot better, especially now that I've seen the interior of Kagiso Lodge. It's beautiful, luxurious, but it's not rigid, or fussy. So, I followed my instincts."

And they were spot-on. Speaking of instincts, his instincts were yelling that they'd be great in bed together...

Tempest-Vane! For God's sake.

"But Naledi might not appreciate her original designs being changed. Maybe I should change them back, tone them done."

No damn way! "For every flower you move, I'll deduct ten grand off your payment." Radd told her, his tone suggesting that she not argue. "You've already lost ten thousand because you moved that one flower."

Brin looked at him, askance before realizing he was teasing. "Okay, okay." She lifted her hands and took a step back.

Brin wrinkled her pretty nose. "I need coffee. And a shower." She sent him an uncertain look. "If you're happy with what I've done, you can tell your pilot to come and collect me."

That would be the best option. She could be gone by noon, and he could spend the rest of the day alone in his favorite place, something he never got to experience anymore. He could simply soak in the essence of Africa and recharge his soul.

That's what he should do, but Radd didn't reach for his phone. Instead, he opted to buy a little time. "Coffee is in the dining room."

Brin followed him to the door, sending him a shy smile when he stood aside to let her walk through the door before him. She seemed surprised by his manners and a little grateful. It was a nice change from the women who either didn't notice or chided him for being gentlemanly, saying that women were perfectly able to open doors for themselves. Of course they were, what the hell did that have anything to do with showing a little bit of courtesy?

Women, would he ever understand them?

Then again, because he was resolved to live his life solo, he would never need to.

Brin looked back into the room, and he gripped her elbow before she could walk back and fiddle with her flowers. "They are fine, Brinley."

Brin looked startled. "How did you know what I was thinking?"

"You have the most expressive eyes in the world," Radd replied, his tone terse. "Come on. Coffee—we could both do with a cup."

Or an intravenous injection containing pure caffeine. And a reality check.

CHAPTER FIVE

BRIN, SITTING IN the passenger seat of a short-wheelbase Land Rover, held her hair back off her face and turned in her seat to look at Radd. Dressed in a red T-shirt, the hem of its sleeves tight around his biceps; old, faded jeans; battered boots; and a Kagiso Lodge cap on his head, he looked the antithesis to the urbane, ruthless businessman with the fearsome reputation she'd met in Cape Town. Light stubble covered his jaw and his broad hands held the steering wheel with complete ease as he whipped the Land Rover down a side road, driving them deeper into the game reserve.

It was obvious that he knew where he was going and how to get there. With each mile they traveled, she sensed his tension ebbing. He loved it here, Brin realized. He'd never admit it, but she sensed this was his happy place.

She didn't have a happy place, not yet. Maybe her shop, if and when she finally opened it, would become the one place where she was totally at ease, utterly in control.

Brin leaned back in her seat, enjoying the early morning sun on her face. She was exhausted, but thrilled with her work last night. On entering the conference room, she'd just wanted to inspect the flowers, map out a plan of action for this morning and see what she was up against. But then she'd picked up a bunch of blue orchids and she'd felt compelled to make a start. One bouquet led to another and soon she was losing time, lost in the moment, immersed in her creativity. Not much could make her forget who and where she was but her craft did...

As did Radd.

When he'd kissed her last night, she'd forgotten why she was at Kagiso, that they were in an open-top vehicle in the middle of the African bush, that she and Radd inhabited completely different worlds. In his arms, she didn't feel like Kerry's little sister, someone who was broke, insecure and still trying to find herself.

In Radd's arms, she felt like the best version of herself.

Brin sighed and rubbed her moist hands on her jeans. He shouldn't be taking up this much mental space. In a couple of hours she would be back in Cape Town and, in two or three more, back in her cottage in Bo Kaap. By tomorrow, or Tuesday, depending on how quickly Radd's funds moved through the banking channels, her money would be in her possession, and she would be free.

Free of the worry of having to go back to Johannesburg with her tail between her legs. Free of the fear of returning to her job as Kerry's assistant—the woman had gone through three already in six months. Free of worrying that she'd eventually fade away, that she'd always be remembered, if she was remembered at all, as being Kerry Riddell's half sister.

But when she returned later, it would be to a Cape Town they both lived in, but where they would no longer connect.

And that was the way it should be.

Because, realistically, there was no chance of her and Radd interacting in an ongoing and meaningful way. Aside from the fact that he was a billionaire and she was broke—okay, she wouldn't be broke for long—they were very different people. He was completely assured and very at ease with himself and his place in the world.

The fact that he constantly dated different woman told her he was commitment-phobic, so she'd never be anything more than a few nights of fun.

But, more than that, Radd was the type of guy she should avoid. He was strong-willed and assertive, a man of very definite opinions. He was also domineering and hard-assed, and she was pretty sure he was the "my-way-or-the-highway" type.

She'd spent the last ten years under the thumb of two very dominating and demanding women, and she wasn't willing to put herself into a situation where she lost her voice, lost herself, again. She was just starting to bloom, slowly understanding who she was and what she stood for. Hooking up with Radd—tough, demanding and dictatorial—would erode all her progress. No, finding herself, restoring her self-belief and confidence, was more important than dropping into a torrid affair with a man who'd discard her when he tired of her.

And he would because, according to the tabloid press, he tired of everyone. When it came to woman, Radd had the attention span of a fruit fly.

So no falling in lust with Radd Tempest-Vane, Riddell. It would be a bad, bad, terrible move.

Falling in love would be the height of stupidity, and she refused to be that girl, the one who "couldn't help herself."

Brin sighed, wondering why she was getting so worked up about something that wouldn't happen. She would be leaving in a couple of hours and soon this would all be a strange memory.

Radd changed gears as he approached a steep hill, idly pointing out a warthog snuffling in the grass next to the road. Brin grinned at the pig, thinking that it was both ugly, cute and very dirty. It looked up at them, snorted and belted into the bush, its tail pointed toward the sky.

They crested the hill and the bush thinned out, revealing a swathe of open savanna. To the left of the road, the grass had been mowed within and around a small, fenced-off area. Brin leaned forward and saw a couple of gravestones beyond the iron fence.

Brin looked at Radd and saw that, while he'd slowed the car to almost a crawl, he was looking straight ahead, as if he were pretending not to notice the graveyard. She placed her hand on his bare, muscled forearm and ignored the heat shimmying up her fingers, along her arm.

"Who is buried there, Radd?"

Radd didn't meet her eyes. "I spoke to one of the rangers this morning, and he said that he saw a pride of young male lions out here yesterday, somewhere just over that ridge. Let's go see if we can spot them," Radd said, a muscle jumping in his clenched jaw.

She loved to see a pride of lions but, strangely, hearing the history of the small graveyard seemed more important.

"I'd rather look at the graveyard," Brin told him. "Stop the car, Radd."

Radd released an aggravated hiss, but he hit the brakes, causing Brin to lurch forward. She braced her hand on the dashboard and lifted her eyebrows at him. "Was that necessary?"

"It's just a graveyard filled with people you don't know!"

Wow, if the temperature of his words had dropped any further, his voice box would've iced over. Brin knew he was trying to intimidate her and that he expected her to cower in her seat and tell him to drive on. The impulse was there, but Radd didn't frighten her. He should, but he didn't. Weird, but true.

It was clear the graveyard was personal and private, so if he didn't want her to look, she'd honor his request.

"Can I take a look around, pay my respects, or would you prefer that I didn't?" Brin asked, keeping her tone nonconfrontational.

Radd whipped his cap off his head, ran his hand through his hair and jammed it back down. He leaned across her and opened her door, so Brin hopped out of the Land Rover and started to walk in the direction of the graveyard. Radd, snapping her name, stopped her progress. "Brin, wait."

Brin watched as she reached behind his seat and pulled out a rifle. He exited the vehicle and slung the weapon over his shoulder. Brin's eyes widened as he walked around to join her, his eyes scanning the bush around him. "Is the rifle really necessary?"

"This is wild land, Brinley, filled with wild animals. Guests are never supposed to leave the vehicle, ever, and if they do, they are on a walking tour, guarded by our armed rangers."

Brin nodded to his weapon. "And do you know how to use that?"

Radd rolled his eyes. "If I didn't, I wouldn't be carrying it."

Designer tailored suits and Hermes ties, Aston Martins and private jets. Battered boots, a cap and a rifle. Who was this man and how many more sides did he have to him? God, he was intriguing.

But, intriguing or not, she was leaving his life in a few hours and that was a good thing. She had work to do, a future to create, and Radd was not only a massive distraction, but also completely wrong for her.

Radd pushed open the small gate leading into the cemetery and gestured Brin to step through. The grass inside the fence was neatly cut and the headstones were free of dust and debris. It was fairly obvious that the area was well looked after.

Brin stopped at the first headstone and stared down at the faded words, unable to make out dates or names. This grave was older than all the others. Brin asked Radd whose it was and when he didn't answer, she turned around, frowning when she saw him standing at the gate, his back to her, his hand rubbing the back of his neck.

Could Radd, normally so implacable and composed, be feeling disconcerted and maybe a little sad? Or maybe even a lot sad.

Moving on, Brin stared down at a bright, newer headstone, reading the words. The date of his birth and death followed the name, Jack Tempest-Vane, and the words *His absence is a silent grief, his life a beautiful memory.* Brin tipped her head to the side, did a mental calculation and quickly realized Jack had to be Radd's brother, and that he'd died when Radd was in his late teens or early twenties.

Brin put her hand on her heart and gently touched his tombstone before moving deeper into the small cemetery, smiling at the cruder gravestones marking the resting place of beloved pets. Then she frowned when she saw one black, flat, unadorned marker glinting in the sun. Brin wandered over to the far corner of the plot.

Gil and Zia Tempest-Vane.

Radd's parents.

They were buried in the family plot but just, tucked away out of sight. Brin dropped to her haunches and brushed twigs off the face of the marker. Black marble, white writing. Just their names and dates of their births and deaths—less than two years ago—were etched into the stone.

Brin placed her hand over her heart as a wave of sadness passed over her. Radd and Digby would've chosen their final resting spot and their choice was a statement in itself. A part of us, but also...

Not.

"Brin, let's *go*."

Brin had a hundred questions for Radd, but his hard face and *Don't ask* expression had the words dying on her lips. Closing the gate behind her, she followed Radd down the path back to the Land Rover and quietly thanked him when he opened the passenger door for her.

After slamming her door shut, Radd stowed the rifle behind the seat and walked to his side of the car. Instead of starting the vehicle, he rummaged behind the seat again and pulled out a thermos. Unscrewing the top, he poured coffee into the thermos' mug, took a sip and handed the mug to Brin.

"Sorry, but we'll have to share."

"This isn't five-star service, Tempest-Vane," Brin teased him, wanting to push his tension away.

"If you were on a proper game drive with one of our rangers, you'd be having breakfast at the edge of a water hole, sitting at a table. You'd have a mimosa in your hand and a croissant on your plate while the chef whipped up a crab, lobster, asparagus and truffle omelet."

Brin took back the cup and looked at him over its rim. "I'm sorry you lost your brother and your parents."

Radd's jaw hardened and his hand gripped the steering wheel, the knuckles white. He stared past her, his expression grim. A minute passed, then another. Brin tightened her grip on the mug and looked back at the grave-yard, accepting that Radd wasn't prepared to discuss his family. And why would he? She was his temporary employee, someone he'd hired to do a job for him, someone he'd shared a kiss with.

A melt-your-socks-off kiss, but still. It meant nothing to him, and it should mean nothing to her. She was trying not to let it.

Whether she was succeeding was up for debate.

"I'm presuming you know something about my parents..."

Brin darted a look at him, unsure how to reply. Sure, she did, who didn't? She'd read about their escapades in the newspapers and celebrity magazines, admiring the way they thumbed their nose at the world.

But she was also old enough to realize her entertainment was Radd's embarrassment. "It must have been hard."

Brin caught the flash of pain that jumped in and out of Radd's eyes. "Hard? Yeah. It was *hard*."

And wasn't that the understatement of the

year? Radd jerked his thumb at the graveyard. "We had a funeral in Paarl, at the family home, but their ashes are over there. It's
a tradition for family members to be buried
here, but we were pissed at them, still are, I
guess. When they died, we weren't talking."

"For how long?"

"The best part of twenty years."

Brin's mouth fell open. "*Wow.*"

Radd shrugged. "To be fair, it wasn't such
a big deal, they weren't around much. And,
God, they were a constant source of humiliation."

Brin wanted to hug him, to pull him into
her arms, but she knew he wouldn't appreciate any displays of sympathy. Look, she
wasn't completely crazy about her own family, but she couldn't imagine never seeing
them again. "You didn't speak to them *once*
in all that time?"

One of Radd's powerful shoulders lifted in
a shrug. "My father left a message for me two
days before the accident, saying they were
coming home, that there was someone they
wanted us to meet."

Brin's curiosity bubbled. "Who was it?"

"God knows. Knowing my parents, it could be their dealer or a sister-wife for my mother. My parents were as mad as a box of frogs," Radd replied, taking the mug of coffee.

"Did you ever look into their papers, check their phone messages, read their emails?" Brin demanded. "Do you have his computer, his diary, his phone? What did you keep?"

Radd's lips twitched at the corners. "Slow down, Nancy Drew. We boxed all his personal effects, the boxes are stored in an attic at Le Bussy, the family home. Look, it was a throwaway comment from a person not renowned for truthfulness. It was probably some stripper he'd met who'd caught his eye."

Brin wrinkled her nose. "Did he ever introduce you to strippers before?

Radd's smile broadened a fraction. "No contact for twenty years, remember? Have some more coffee…" Brin took the cup back, sipped.

"You have an active imagination," Radd continued. "I'm convinced my father was just blowing smoke, he was really good at doing that."

"But…"

That muscle in his jaw jumped again, his expression hardened and the strong hand on the wheel tightened. Then, Radd glanced at her and his fabulous blue eyes were a deep, dark, intense blue. And filled with pain. And guilt. And a little anger.

She'd pushed too far and he was closing down.

"I'm asking you never to repeat what I just told you, Brinley," Radd stated, his voice colder than a dip in the Bering Sea.

"You have my word." Brin passed the coffee mug to him and watched as he took a long sip, briefly closing his eyes. Handing her the mug again, he pulled his sunglasses from off his T-shirt and slipped them over his face, likely more to shield his eyes than to block out the glare of the sun.

"Shall we go look for those lions?" Brin asked, changing the subject, and relief flashed across his face.

"Absolu—" Radd's reply was interrupted by the jarring, strident tones of his phone ringing, and he lifted his buttock to pull his phone out of the back pocket of his jeans.

"Those things don't belong in the bush," Brin muttered, annoyed by the interruption.

Radd sent her his sexy half-smile, half-smirk. The one that always warmed her. "I couldn't agree more. But, unfortunately, I'm not on holiday and they are a necessary evil." Radd lifted the device to his ear and briefly lifted his hand to point toward a large tree, and a massive antelope standing in the tree's shade.

"Male kudu...hey, Dig."

Brin and the kudu exchanged interested glances as the vehicle slowed down to a crawl. She could hear Digby's voice and, though his words were indistinguishable, judging by the horrified expression on Radd's face, he was the bearer of bad news. And, by the way, Radd looked at her, it involved her. Oh, crap, could Radd have found out her tenuous connection to Naledi? And did it matter? The flowers were done, and she was leaving; Naledi would never find out.

It wasn't, shouldn't be, an issue.

"Okay, well, thanks for letting me know. I'll call you in the morning to make further arrangements."

Radd disconnected the call and gently banged the expensive device against the steering wheel as the vehicle rolled to a stop.

"Problem?" Brin asked.

"Yeah. The pilot called Digby this morning, he picked up a problem when he was flying back yesterday. The technicians are working on it, but the plane won't be able to pick you up today and the repairs will take a few days, maybe more."

Brin felt cold, then hot, then cold again. Oh, crap, no.

"The Radebe's have agreed to use their own jet, which will leave Johannesburg, collect them in Cape Town, offload them here and return to Johannesburg." Radd placed his forearm on the steering wheel and faced her, her expression troubled. "So, what the hell do I do with you?"

Color drained from Brin's face and Radd noticed her trembling hand. Whipping the coffee cup from her grasp, he tossed the liquid onto the veld grass and screwed the cup back onto the thermos, watching a dozen emotions jump in and out of her eyes.

A few minutes back, when they were talking about his parents—a topic he never discussed, not even with Digby—he'd felt like he was sitting on a hot griddle, but it was obvious he'd swapped places with Brin. Later, he'd try and work out why he'd revealed so much to Brin and why he felt comfortable opening up to her, but right now, he needed to focus on this latest hitch in his plans.

Brin bit her bottom lip. The plane's delay was an inconvenience, but it didn't warrant her deer-in-the-headlights expression. "Do you have somewhere to be tomorrow?"

"No, I mean, yes! Yes, I have to go back to Cape Town!" Brin quickly replied, her eyes sliding away as her cheeks turned a pretty shade of pink. Damn, she was a really bad liar.

"A job? A doctor's appointment? Lunch? A date?" He narrowed his eyes, inexplicably annoyed at the idea of her seeing someone else.

"Yes, a doctor's appointment and a date."

Lies number two and three.

Radd tapped his index finger on the knob of the gear lever. "I told you that I don't like lies."

"You told me you don't like secrets and surprises," Brin pointed out.

She was splitting hairs, because lies and secrets led to surprises. "So, why are you lying about needing to be somewhere tomorrow?"

"I can't stay here, Radd. I just can't," Brin replied, still not able to meet his eyes.

"It's a luxurious resort, not a jail cell, Brinley," Radd retorted. "What's the problem with you staying and leaving with me on Friday?"

Brin stared down at her intertwined hands, her lower lip between her teeth. "I need to get back to Cape Town, Radd. You promised I'd be back today. Can I hire a jet or, more realistically, another—smaller—plane?"

Damn, she really didn't want to stay. Radd felt the stabbing pain in his chest and frowned. Could he be feeling hurt? And if he was, what the hell was wrong with him?

"Sure, but it's expensive. And I haven't done your transfer yet and that amount of cash will take a couple of days to clear." He named a figure that had her eyes widening. "Do you have that sort of cash lying around?"

Brin shook her head. "No."

He didn't think so.

"I could hire a car..."

What the hell? Why was she so determined to get away, to leave him? And wasn't he feeling like a complete idiot for talking to her about his parents, for opening up?

So stupid.

"Brinley, what is the problem? You obviously don't have any commitments back in Cape Town. You're staying in a luxurious villa at one of the world's best safari operations. We have world-class chefs, an extensive wine list and a spa. Consider the extra few days a holiday, a bonus for doing such a fabulous job on the flowers."

Brin pushed her curls back, pleasure at his compliment in her light, bright eyes. "You really like the flowers, don't you?"

"I told you I did, didn't I?" Radd snapped, confused by her lack of confidence. Why couldn't she see how good she was and why did she seem to need assurance? This woman was a constant contradiction; he couldn't figure her out.

And if she stayed, he'd have a couple more days to do that.

And more opportunities to get her into bed.

Because really, that's what he wanted. He wanted to explore her long, slim body with its subtle curves, feel the weight of her breasts in his hand, pull her nipple into his mouth. Explore all those soft, secret, wonderful, feminine places he adored...

While they were both stuck in Kagiso they could indulge in a no commitment, no promises affair... Short on drama, but long on pleasure.

But Radd knew he couldn't push her, that if he did, she'd find a way to haul her very pretty ass back to Cape Town.

"Tell me about your guests?"

It was a strange question and not one he'd expected. But, because it was a little step in the right direction, he quickly answered her. "Naledi Radebe, obviously, and her parents, Vincent and June Radebe." He racked his brain, trying to remember who else would be attending the pre-wedding week. He mentioned a couple of names, and Brin didn't react.

"You didn't mention the groom," Brin pointed out.

"Apparently he's on a film set and the movie

only wraps up on Wednesday night. He and the best man will fly in on Thursday night. It's a sore point and the bride is not happy."

Brin's shoulders dropped an inch. "And do you expect me to spend a lot of time with them?"

God, *no*. "Hell, *I* don't expect to spend a lot of time with them," he replied. "I might have to join them one night for dinner, maybe for a drink occasionally, but this is a family holiday. They don't want me there all the time. And I, most definitely, do not want to spend a lot of time with them."

"Not your type of people?" Brin asked.

Few were. He far preferred to be on his own, or with Digby. "It's a business relationship, and I like to keep clear boundaries."

Those boundaries were important, in business and in his personal life. *Can you try and remember that, Tempest-Vane, and stop talking to her about your family?* Radd looked at his watch. "So, are you staying or going, Brinley?"

Brin twisted her lips, obviously deep in thought. "I'll stay, if I can keep a low profile. And I don't want you telling the bride, or any of the wedding party, that I did the flowers. Tell them that you hired a designer from Cape Town and that she's already left."

"Why on earth would I do that?" Radd demanded. The bouquets were stunning, why wouldn't she want to take the credit for them? "Look, the Radebes might not be my cup of tea, but they are influential and if they know that you did the flowers, they might use you again."

Brin shook her head. "Don't tell them, Radd. Please?"

If this was her attitude toward potential business, then she would never make it. But that, Radd reminded himself, wasn't his problem. Brin would be out of his life soon, a lovely memory. If he ever thought about her at all.

He only wanted her in his life for the next few days. And, judging by his past encounters with the fairer sex, five days of her constant company was about three days too many. He got claustrophobic and irritated when he was in someone's company for too long; Brin wouldn't be any different. And, let's be honest here—because he always was—if they didn't end up sleeping together, it was going to be a goddamn long week.

Because, *people.*

As much as he wished things could be different, that he had a normal approach to relationships, the truth was that he was the product of two of the most dysfunctional people in the world. His parents not only had a wide-open marriage, but they'd had no loyalty to each other or to the rest of their family. Their pleasures and gratification—sexual, financial and emotional—always came first.

But weirdly, despite the numerous affairs on both sides, his parents had been insanely jealous. He recalled vicious fights, the throwing of crystal and china, of shoes and handbags, his mother screaming and his father's mocking responses. He recalled rooms being trashed and walls punched and, in the morning, when it all was over, he remembered lines of coke on tables.

He had no idea what a good marriage looked like; his parents were his only reference.

So much about relationships rattled him. He was terrified he'd not only lose control and his temper, but also his dignity, so he avoided anyone who made his heart accelerate, his breath catch. If he liked a woman a little too much, he dropped her quickly, walking away without a second glance.

Because what if he took a chance on love and it backfired? What if his partner ran to the press after a fight? What if she had an affair and the press found out? What if she…

Radd shuddered. God, no! He'd lived through that scrutiny as a child and teenager and he would not, ever, go through that again. The only way to guarantee that was not to get involved with anyone, ever.

But none of his mental ramblings had anything to do with Brin's flowers. And it was her choice whether to take the credit or not.

"Fine," Radd told her.

"And I can keep a low profile when your other guests arrive?" Brin asked, and something in her expression made him pause. Why was she so determined not to interact, to keep her distance? Naledi was a social butterfly and her face was instantly recognizable, but Brin had no interest in making her acquaintance. It was unusual, and Radd didn't trust unusual.

"Is there something you're not telling me?"

Brin shrugged and rubbed her fingertips over her brow, her hand effectively hiding her eyes from him. "It's been a long and confusing day and it's not even seven yet. I'm really tired."

"Yet I still don't know whether you are staying or going."

Brin scrubbed her face with her hands before slumping in her seat. "I'm not going to lie, I don't have the money to pay deposits to hire a plane or a car. So you…" she drilled a finger into his chest "…need to pay me."

"And I will when I get the chance," Radd replied.

Brin hauled in a huge breath. "Provided I don't have to join or interact with the wedding party, and if I can stay in the background, then I'll stay."

Radd worked hard to keep his expression inscrutable, to stop himself from doing an air pump. "Good." No, it was damned excellent.

Brin gestured to the bush beyond their car. "Do you think we can go back? I'm really tired and would love a nap." She sent him a mischievous grin that tightened his pants and ignited flames in his stomach. "And, seeing that I'm now your guest, I'd like that crab, lobster and truffle omelet."

Radd grinned and accelerated away. When she forgot to be insecure, Ms. Riddell could be quite bossy. He rather liked it.

CHAPTER SIX

LATER THAT EVENING, Brin walked from the dining area of the main lodge onto its expansive deck and plopped down on one of the wide two-person loungers, kicking off her shoes to swing her bare feet up onto the cushion. Leaning back, she tipped her head up, sighing at the swish of stars making up the Milky Way.

"I can't get enough of this sky."

"It's pretty impressive," Radd agreed. Brin pulled her eyes away from the sky to watch him gracefully walk across the deck, holding a bottle of red wine and two glasses. Stopping next to her lounger, he dashed wine into the glasses while kicking off his flip-flops. He'd pulled on a light, hooded sweatshirt to counter the slight chill in the air but still wore the cargo shorts he'd changed into after their game drive earlier that morning.

"Shift over," Radd told her and dropped down into the space she created. His shoulder pressed into hers, his thigh lay alongside hers, and Brin felt like he'd plugged her into an electric substation. He was so big, so solid, so very masculine...

Untamed and a little intimidating, like the land he so loved.

Radd handed her a glass of red wine and Brin placed it on the floor next to her, in easy reach. He placed his arm behind his head, sighed and look upwards, and Brin could almost feel the tension leaving his body.

Radd relaxing had happened in increments all day, a sigh here, a roll of the shoulders there. Kagiso was good for him, Brin decided. No, Kagiso was great for him.

"It's not often I'm here on my own, and I forget how much I love it when it's empty," Radd said, his soft words echoing her thoughts.

"Except that you are not alone, I'm here," Brin pointed out.

"But you're surprisingly restful company, Brinley Riddell." Radd turned his head to look at her and his small smile made her stomach flip over. And over again. "You don't feel the need to fill silences with chatter, you're happy to be quiet. That's pretty unusual. Why is that?"

Brin lifted her wineglass and took a sip. "Probably because I have a sister who dominates every conversation and a mother who encourages her."

"And your dad?"

"Stepdad," Brin corrected him. "He's sweet but quiet. He's been in my life since I was a three, but we've never really bonded, I guess."

Brin felt his eyes on her face but didn't look at him, choosing instead to track a satellite moving across the sky. "Why not?"

"Because my mom fell pregnant with my sister and, from that moment on, it became all about her," Brin admitted. "I was never in any doubt about who their favorite child was."

Radd didn't respond and Brin appreciated his silence, there was nothing worse than trite sympathy. Not that she believed Radd could, or would, be trite but...still.

"If it makes you feel any better, my parents didn't have favorites. They disliked us all equally."

Brin rolled onto her side, resting her head in her hand. The amazing sky couldn't compete with this fascinating man. "Why do you think they had kids if they were so uninterested in being parents?"

A cynical smile touched Radd's mouth. "That might be because my great-grandfather, my father's grandfather, set up a trust fund in the fifties, when the Tempest-Vanes were seriously rolling in cash—"

"As opposed to how poor you are now," Brin interjected, her tongue literally in her cheek.

Radd's chuckle at her quip warmed her. "Brat. But I'm talking about family money, not what Dig and I made since my parents lost everything." Radd lifted his wineglass, took a sip and placed it back on the floor. "Anyway, my father was the only T-V descendant—Great-Grandfather's other son died in his teens and his daughter didn't marry or have kids—so it was up to my father to restock the family tree. Great-Grandfather told my father that he'd give him two million for every male child they produced."

Brin wasn't sure how to respond to that blatant, old-fashioned misogyny and finally settled on: "Nice of you lot to cooperate and be male."

Radd's chuckle danced over her skin. "The first and only thing we did right," he said, and his lack of emotion saddened Brin.

She risked putting her hand on his chest, somewhere in the region of his heart. "Scale of one to ten…how bad was it?"

Radd's chest lifted and fell in a jerky movement, and then his hand clasped hers, pushing her flat palm against his chest. "Honestly, about a five. I mean, we weren't beaten or neglected, we had everything we needed. We went to an expensive boarding school and we were happy there. We spent a lot of time here at Kagiso. As long as we were together, we were okay. And Jack was five years older, so he stood between the parents and us."

Brin shifted down and placed her head against Radd's shoulder, happy to hold his hand in the moonlight. "And then he died. How?"

"Brain aneurysm," Radd replied. "It was a shock."

Now that was the understatement of the year, because Brin could see the devastation in his eyes. "I'm sure it was. And around the same time, you divorced your parents."

"Divorce... That's a good way to put it," Radd mused. His hand tightened and Brin winced, but didn't pull away. Whatever he was thinking about was painful, and she knew the wound was still raw.

"Did you sell their art and car collections?"

Radd shook his head. "Everything they owned, including their property and cash, and two massive life insurance policies, was put into a trust. Neither of us is a trustee or a beneficiary."

Brin frowned. "Who is?"

"That's the question. We don't know, we can't find out and frankly, we don't much care."

She thought he did, a little. But something in his voice had her cocking her head, questioning. "Why do I think you know more about that than you are saying?"

Brin smiled at his shock. "How the hell do you know that?" he demanded.

She shrugged. "Just a guess. Can you tell me?"

Radd hesitated. "I have no proof, but I suspect the person he wanted us to meet and the beneficiary of that trust is the same person."

"Could be," Brin agreed. "But it would be hell to prove."

"Yep."

"Look, I know your parents were...unconventional, but can you tell me what caused you to divorce them? Can you trust me with that information or is it too personal?"

"Jesus, Brin, that's a hell of a question."

The night wrapped them in its soft embrace and Brin couldn't help dropping a kiss on his shoulder, hoping, in a small way, to give him an anchor while horrible memories battered him from every side. Because she did not doubt that, whatever it was that caused that final break, it had to be truly horrible.

Radd eventually started to speak, and Brin held her breath. "Digby and I were used to being teased about their antics, about their rock-and-roll lifestyle. We learned to either ignore it, roll with it or mock it. It helped that we were popular at school and good sportsmen. But, God, the stories never stopped. It felt like every week something about them hit the headlines…"

It hadn't been that bad but, to their kids, it must have seemed like it.

"We genuinely believed that the press just reported on the stories but, at Jack's funeral, we realized Gil and Zia had an unholy pact with the tabloids, and they were the source of most of the exposés. They loved the attention."

Brin winced.

"Jack died and photographs of his funeral—Digby and I insisted that it was to be a small, very intimate and very private affair—were leaked to the paparazzi, and we lost it. We were livid. We quickly worked out that our parents were the only people who could've given the photos to the press and when we confronted them, they confirmed it."

Brin blinked away her tears and wished she could dig his parents up and, well, *punch* them. She wasn't a violent person, but she'd happily step into the ring with Radd's par-

144 HOW TO UNDO THE PROUD BILLIONAIRE

ents. She couldn't believe they thought it was okay to profit off their oldest son's death...

"After that, we didn't have any contact with them," Radd concluded on a small shrug.

Brin buried her face against the ball of his shoulder, her body shaking with anger. Her mother wouldn't win any prizes in the "best mommy" competition but, compared to Radd's parents, she was a saint. Her heart ached for the two boys who raised themselves.

Brin felt Radd pull away from her and, when his hand cupped her cheek, she opened her eyes to find his face inches from hers, his expression concerned. His thumb swiped her cheekbone and his breath caressed her cheek. "Are you okay?"

Brin shook her head. "No, I'm so damn angry I want to clout something!" Brin retorted.

"Why are you... *Oh.* You're angry for me?"

Why did he sound so bemused, like that wasn't possible? Brin sat up, pushed her hair and slapped her arms over her chest. "No, I'm not angry, I'm livid. What was wrong with them? How dare they do that? Are you freaking *kidding* me? That is insane and horrible and—"

Radd shoved a glass of wine into her hand. "Sip." Brin took a large gulp and sighed when the soft, complex liquid slid down her throat.

"And, while I appreciate your reaction, it all happened a long time ago," he added.

"Still…"

Brin sucked in a deep breath and, knowing that she needed to lighten the atmosphere, that they were wading into deep, dark emotional waters—a place she couldn't afford to visit and if she did, couldn't stay long—she dredged up a teasing smile. "You're thirty-six. Damn, you're old."

Radd's eyes narrowed at her, but she caught the flash of relief, in his eyes. They'd gone too deep, too fast, and he wanted to swim back to shore. "Who are you calling old, wretch?"

"You."

"You do know that there is a pool about six feet from us and I can drop you in it?" Radd threatened.

"You wouldn't dare…"

Brin squealed when, in one fluid movement, he stood up and lifted her up against his chest, without, she had to admit, any strain at all. Radd walked her over to the pool and swung her away from his body.

"Radd, no!" Brin really didn't want to go for a swim in that still, cold water. She released a wild laugh and tightened her grip around his neck. "My hair takes forever to dry, it's too cold and I'm sorry I called you old!"

Radd's fingers dug into her ribs and she squirmed as he tickled her. "How sorry are you?" he demanded, a huge smile making him look ten years younger.

"Very." Brin's eyes connected with his and his arms tightened, pulling her tighter to his chest. *He is so warm*, Brin thought, *so strong*. Brin saw his eyes leave hers to look at her mouth and, when their eyes reconnected, she saw that desire, hot and heavy, had replaced his amusement.

"You are so damn beautiful," he rasped.

Brin knew that he was going to kiss her and that she was going to let him. How could she resist? And why should she? A sexy man held her in his arms, the night was stunning and they were alone…

"Children, it's good to see you playing nicely but, Radd, I need to talk to you."

Okay, so not alone.

Brin slid down Radd's body and, when her feet touched the ground, she turned to see Mari standing at the entrance to the lodge, looking stressed. Radd took a step away from her, ran his hand over his jaw and nodded. But Brin heard his low, under-the-breath curse at Mari's timing.

Yep, it sucked.

Radd walked over to the lounger, picked up the bottle of wine and the glasses, and placed them on the closest wrought iron table. "Come on over, Mari. And bring a glass for some wine."

When Mari turned away, he handed Brin her glass and she shuddered when his fingers brushed hers. She lifted her glass in a toast, her hand trembling. "Thanks for not dropping me in the pool, old man."

Radd's hand shot out, gripped the back of her neck to pull her closer and his mouth, hot, hard and insistent, swiped over hers. A second, maybe two later, he lifted his head and his eyes glittered with frustration, lust and a healthy dose of humor. "Oh, I still can. And before the week is out, I probably will."

Brin had the feeling that he wasn't only talking about an unscheduled dip.

Brin watched as Radd flipped on the outside lights and the atmosphere on the veranda changed from sensual to sensible. Slipping on her flip-flops, Brin started to excuse herself but, before she could, Radd waved her to a chair.

Radd leaned against the railing behind Brin, his wineglass resting against his bicep. "What's the problem, Mari?"

Mari crossed her elegant legs, hauled in a deep breath and tried to smile. "Apparently your guests will be here for breakfast, not afternoon tea."

Radd frowned. "Okay, that's not a huge problem, is it?"

Mari's deep brown eyes reflected her frustration. "No, that's easily handled."

Radd moved to take a seat next to Brin, and Radd placed his hand on her arm. "Ready for dinner?"

As if she could think of food when he was

touching her. Sparks ran up and down her arm and warmth settled in her stomach and between her legs. Really, her reaction to him was instantaneous and inconvenient.

"I still need a little more of your time, Radd. Sorry, Brin."

"Do you want me to leave?" Brin asked.

Mari smiled at her. "That's not necessary."

Radd stroked her arm before lifting his hand off her skin. He placed his forearms on the table, his focus shifting to Mari. Mari started to run through the coming week, the guests and their preferences. Brin was impressed by their no-notes discussion, both owner and manager had all the facts at their fingertips.

Brin admired Mari's ability to answer Radd's rapid questions, but she was very impressed by Radd's insightful and detailed questions.

He deep dived into the operation, and Brin's eyes bounced from Mari's delicate features to Radd's masculine face, frequently losing track of what they were discussing.

She'd expected Radd to only have a surface-based knowledge of Kagiso. He was, after all, the not-here-that-often owner, and he had many fingers in many business pies. But Radd could, at a moment's notice, drop into Mari's position and run the lodge with precision and assurance.

Radd caught her stare and a small frown creased his eyebrows. "Why are you looking at me like that?"

Brin lifted one shoulder, a little embarrassed to be caught out. "Um, I'm just impressed at how much you know about the day-to-day running of the lodge."

"It is my lodge," Radd pointed out.

"I know but I thought, because you own so many other businesses, that you'd oversee the place and leave the details to your management team," Brin said.

Mari laughed, her eyes dancing. "Radd is a control freak, Brin. Actually, I'm surprised that he didn't spend the night looking over your shoulder, telling you where to put each individual flower in your arrangements."

"I'm not that bad," Radd protested.

"Yeah, you are," Marri told him, patting his hand affectionately. She smiled at Brin.

"Even as a kid, he was incredibly bossy. The only person Radd ever listened to was Jack."

Brin placed her chin in the palm of her hand, watching the interaction between the two. That they knew each other well wasn't in dispute, and Brin was both glad and sad—weird to be both at the same time—that her instincts about Radd's controlling personality were spot-on. Glad because who didn't want to be right, and sad because, well, if there was a man she could see herself becoming entangled with then Radd Tempest-Vane was right at the top of that list.

Attraction played a huge part, but she also liked the man, which was unexpected. Then again, she occasionally liked her mom and sister, too. But they were, in their entirety, bad for her. Radd would be, as well.

While she enjoyed their conversation earlier, loved seeing a glimpse of the real man behind the ruthless veneer he wore, she wasn't under any illusions it *meant* anything. Radd wasn't looking for anything permanent, neither was she.

But, while resisting Rich Radd, the implacable billionaire, was easy, she was crazy attracted to the flawed, sexy, sweet man she'd glimpsed earlier. Resisting that Radd was going to be as hard as hell.

But that wasn't who Radd was all the time; Real Radd was hard, tough and uncompromising. Real Radd would overwhelm and dilute her...

"Oh, and they've added an extra person to the party," Mari added.

Radd's frown pulled Brin's attention back to the conversation. "What?"

Mari rolled her expressive eyes. "One of the bridesmaids changed her plans and Mrs. Radebe is demanding we accommodate her."

Radd pinched the bridge of his nose and muttered a harsh curse. "These people are going to drive me insane."

Brin caught the flash of uncertainty that flashed across Mari's face. "An additional guest is going to require an additional room. With Brinley in a villa, we're short of beds."

Right, the universe was trying to send Brin a message. She needed to go back to Cape Town, needed to leave Kagiso and remove herself from Radd's orbit. It would've been lovely to spend the balance of the week enjoying the six-star resort, but if Mari needed the space for paying guests, she'd have to vacate. Radd would have to find a way to return her to the city now.

And again, she felt both glad and sad.

Radd stared at her, his eyes boring into hers. In those inky eyes, she saw a variety of emotions, most of which she couldn't identify. He seemed to be weighing his options, turning over possibilities, looking for pros and cons.

"There's Digby's villa."

Radd shook his head. "No, Mari, out of the question. When we established the lodge, Dig and I agreed that we'd never hire our personal residences to guests. That's his personal space and it's not happening." Radd turned to Brin. "Digby's villa is next to mine." A barely there, almost satisfied smile touched the corners of Radd's lips, and Brin frowned, wondering what he was up to. "Brin can move into my villa."

Uh, *really*? "And where will you sleep?" she demanded. Radd's smile deepened and his eyes heated. Brin, seeing the answer in his eyes—*with you, obviously*—quickly shook her head. "That's not a good idea."

Before Radd could reply, Mari pushed her chair back and quietly excused herself. Brin, not wanting to break eye contact with Radd, didn't acknowledge her leaving and neither, Brin noticed, did her boss.

"I'm not sleeping with you, Radd," Brin told him, annoyed that her voice sounded a little shaky. And not very assertive.

Radd nodded. "Okay."

Brin didn't trust his immediate agreement. "Look, I'm adult enough to realize that we are hectically attracted to each other, but I'm not the type to fall into bed with hot billionaires."

"Okay."

"Stop saying that!" Brin snapped.

Radd leaned back in his chair, stretched out his legs and linked his hands on his flat stomach, looking supremely relaxed. "What do you think is going to happen if you move into my villa, Brin?"

"We're two unattached, single people who are attracted to each other," Brin replied, annoyed. "What the hell do you think is going to happen? Do you think we'll spend all our time playing tiddlywinks? We'll end up having sex."

"Do you want to have sex with me?"

How could he sound so relaxed, like they were discussing the weather? "I'm not answering that question."

"So, that's a yes, then."

"It's not a yes!" Brin snapped.

"Then it's a no?"

Brin refused to look at him, wanting to lie but unable to. So she kept quiet, hoping for a hole to open up and suck her into another vortex, a different paradigm. She waited, but nothing happened and she eventually, what seemed like years later, looked at Radd.

He still looked relaxed and worse, amused.

"You are so damn annoying." Brin pushed her curls back off her face and cupped her hand behind her neck, feeling out of her depth and a little emotional. God, at times like these she wished she were more like Kerry, sophisticated and cool, able to give as good as she got.

People like Radd and her sister could run rings around her without moving at all.

The amusement faded from Radd's eyes and his expression turned serious. "You're seriously upset about this."

Well, yes. She didn't like feeling as though she was the ditsy hen and he the sly fox.

Radd sat up straight, leaned forward and placed his hand on her knee. "Look at me, Brinley." Radd waited for her to meet his eyes before speaking again. "I don't want you to leave Kagiso, not yet. And yes, we need your room and a solution is for you to move in with me. But that's all I'm asking you to do."

"But—" Brin waved a hand between them "—you know."

"Do I want to sleep with you? Hell, yes. Does your moving into my place guarantee that's going to happen? Hell, no." Radd tapped his finger on her knee when her eyes slid away. "Keep looking at me, Brinley. You're in control here, you're calling the shots. Would I like to see, taste and have you? Sure, I would. You're a gorgeous woman and making love to you would be a privilege. But that's your decision, always. If you're not interested or not ready, I get it, and I'll either sleep on the couch or in the hammock on the veranda."

"You will?"

Radd looked annoyed at her questioning his motives. "I'm hard-assed and demanding. I'm abrupt and reticent, but I don't force, coerce or bully women into sleeping with me." Radd ran his fingers through his hair. "But if you don't feel comfortable, if you don't trust me enough, then I'll make a call and hire a plane to get you home by nightfall."

If he'd tried to persuade her, if he'd brushed off her concerns or dismissed them out of hand, then Brin would've taken him up on his offer to get her home, but because he did neither, because she instinctively trusted his integrity, she glanced down and stroked her finger over the raised veins in his broad, masculine hand.

"You must think I am desperately naive and old-fashioned," Brin quietly commented.

Radd took a moment to answer her. "I think you are refreshing and out of the ordinary. I don't often invite people to share my personal space, Brinley. Neither do I talk about my past, but I like talking to you. I like you.

And if all I can get is your company, then I'll take it."

Was he being sarcastic? Was he just saying that to get his own way? To manipulate her into doing what he wanted her to do?

Brin looked into his eyes, steady and strong, and the honesty reflected in those inky blue depths reassured her. She allowed her suspicions to drain away. She believed him but, more than that, she trusted him. Trusted him to keep his word, to not push her, to respect her boundaries.

Boundaries that were, let's be honest, not that solid, barriers that could easily be decimated.

"You'll sleep on the couch or in the hammock?"

"I will." Then Radd smiled and her heart flipped over. "Unless you invite me to share *my* bed."

Radd stood up abruptly and held out his hand for her to take. "I'll get Chef to deliver our dinner, and your luggage, to my villa. We can eat on the deck, it overlooks a watering hole."

He was too self-confident by half, a little

presumptuous and a lot arrogant, but that didn't stop Brin from sliding her hand into his and allowing him to lead her out of the dining room.

The next morning, Radd looked around his private villa, thinking that this open-plan space had always been his refuge, the one place he felt utterly at home.

He'd personally designed the spacious two-roomed, open-plan villa and some of his most treasured pieces of furniture had ended up here. In the corner sat his grandfather's desk, above it on the wall were family photographs from the original farmhouse, demolished shortly after the new owners took possession of the property.

The enormous bed came from Le Bussy, the wine farm in Paarl, brought over by the first Tempest-Vane to arrive on the subcontinent.

There were antique fishing rods on another wall, all used by generations of Tempest-Vanes, and the four-seater sofa and its two matching wingback chairs, restuffed and recovered, were all old but supremely comfortable. Beyond the bedroom was a massive bathroom, complete with a slipper bath and his and hers basins. Floor-to-ceiling doors opened up onto an outdoor shower and Radd loved nothing more than to stand beneath the hard spray, looking up into the branches of an ancient shepherd tree shielding the villa from the harsh African sun. There was something incredibly sexy and primal about showering outside, especially at night when the stars hung so low he felt he could pluck them from the sky and hold them in his hand.

He could easily imagine standing in that space with a naked Brin, licking droplets of water off her breasts, her flat stomach, running his hands down her long legs, tipping her head back to suckle on her elegant neck...

God, he couldn't think about her like that, naked, while she lay on his bed, gently sleeping.

Radd tipped his face up to the sun, enjoying the still pleasant heat, and whipped off his T-shirt, enjoying the prickles of sunshine on his shoulders and back.

God, he loved Kagiso.

This was the place where he recharged his

batteries, where he could spend hours looking over his land or at the water hole, completely content to while away the hours on his own, watching the light change and the animals wandering into his line of sight.

Kagiso, particularly this villa—with its wide veranda, comfortable seating, a telescope and a plunge pool—was the place he ran to when life became a little too real, a bit harsh, the demands of business overwhelming.

Here, on his own, he could breathe, he could relax, he could simply be.

This space was his bolt hole and, to an extent, sacred. It wasn't a space he shared, not even with Digby, as close as they were.

Radd stood at the railing of the veranda and turned his back on the water hole to look into the room, past the lounge area to the massive bed, draped in mosquito netting against a stone wall. Brin lay on her side, her hands under her cheek, deep in sleep.

God, she was beautiful. Fresh, lovely, unusual. And she was in his space, in this place that he regarded at his little piece of paradise.

Radd watched her sleep for another minute or two before forcing himself to pull his eyes off her delicate profile, to stop himself from tracing the curve of her lips, the arch of her cheekbones, from counting the number of freckles on her nose and cheeks.

She was unlike anyone he'd ever met before, feminine and strong, yet curiously vulnerable and more than a little sweet.

He wasn't normally attracted to sweet woman, to vulnerable innocents. He didn't have the time and energy to dance around them, to watch his words, to reign in his forthright observations or to measure his words. Yet, despite her softness, he didn't feel the need to censure himself around Brinley, she'd proved that she could handle him at his most irritable and demanding.

He admired her pride, the fact that she was not intimidated by his wealth, success or power. He enjoyed her sly sense of humor and was constantly surprised that she seemed to get him. She was unlike any woman he'd encountered before.

And last night he'd opened up to her, told her things about his past and family he'd never discussed with anyone but Digby. And he was *not* okay with that.

What the hell had he been thinking?

Nobody but the two brothers knew that Gil and Zia left all their worldly assets to a trust, that they'd sold photographs from Jack's funeral to the press. And, because he'd been seduced by a sweet-smelling woman and a warm, star-filled night, there was always a chance that tomorrow, or the day after, or next week, or next month, these nuggets of information could land in the gossip columns, as another episode in the Tempest-Vane saga.

Radd felt the cold fringes of panic claw up his throat and his fingers curled around the railing, slowly turning white. He didn't think Brin would go to the press, didn't think she was the type, but he should not have taken the chance. What the hell had he been thinking?

Dammit. He should've got her to sign a nondisclosure agreement...

Yeah, fantastic plan, Tempest-Vane. She'd take that well. Not.

Radd tipped his head up to the sky, wishing he wasn't so distrustful, so god-awful cynical. But his employing her, and his attraction to her, had happened so damn fast he was still trying to catch up.

The only thing he could do, what he would do, was to keep his mouth shut from this point onwards.

Radd rested his arms on the railing of the balcony and stared down at the water below him, uncomfortable with his mental ramblings, his deep dive into his psyche. He had to reign this emotion in, go back into his cool cocoon where little touched him. He was here, at Kagiso, to get Vincent Radebe to sign the final papers that would give them ownership of the mine and, when that was done, they'd launch the PR and rebranding campaign.

He had to stick to things he could control and Brinley Riddell, with her light eyes and soft curls, was not on that list.

He'd best remember that.

CHAPTER SEVEN

BRIN, SITTING AT the dining table on the deck of Radd's villa, her bare feet up on the railing and a coffee cup in her hand, turned at the sound of the door opening. Her heart picked up speed, as it always did when it was in the same room as Radd, and she whipped around to see him walking into the villa, tossing his hat onto the king-size bed.

Today he was dressed in the bottle green polo shirt all the game rangers wore, khaki shorts and boots, and he looked as wild and as tough as the land stretched below them.

Radd caught her eyes, smiled and her stomach joined her heart's around-her-body race. "Morning."

"Hi, how was your game drive? See anything interesting?"

Radd took the seat opposite her, leaned across the table and snagged a piece of her jam smeared croissant. He chewed, swallowed and took the coffee cup from her hand and drained the contents before handing her empty cup back.

She lifted her eyebrows at him.

"Relax, fresh coffee, croissants and fruit are on its way," Radd told her, bending down to unlace his boots. "The drive through the park was awesome, you should've come with us."

"There wasn't space," Brin reminded him. The wedding party filled every seat in the vehicle, and Naledi and her friends weren't the type of people she'd get up before dawn to spend time with. She couldn't complain though, Radd had taken her for a drive on both Monday and last night, Tuesday, leaving his game rangers to look after the guests.

"I like it when we're on our own," Brin quietly admitted.

"Me, too," Radd softly replied.

Brin turned his head to look at him and her breath caught in her throat at the desire blazing in his eyes. His hair was ruffled, his jaw thick with stubble and as sexy as sin. Brin felt a tremble roll through her and she couldn't help licking her lips, wishing his was covering hers, his tongue in her mouth, his hand pushing her thighs apart.

Oh, God, she wanted him, here in the sunlight at just past eight in the morning...

And, judging by his clenched fist resting on the table and the flush on his cheekbones, he wanted her, too. Brin looked from him to the daybed where Radd slept, hanging from chains in the corner of the veranda. It was big enough for an orgy—hammock, her ass—and she wondered if she was brave enough to say something, anything, to get him to join her on that wide surface.

Are you ready for that, Brin Riddell? Ready for a hot affair that would end the day after next, when they returned to Cape Town? She didn't know, she wasn't sure...

Brin pulled her eyes off him and searched for something to say to break the tension. "Did you see anything interesting?" she asked.

Radd ate another piece of her croissant before attacking his other boot. "A leopard, a pangolin, a herd of elephants."

Nice. "I've never seen a pangolin."

"They are pretty rare," Radd said, sitting up

and, copying her, put his bare feet up on the railing. "They are the most traded animals in the world and are highly, highly endangered. I tried to explain that to the bride and her maids, but they weren't that interested. They spent most of the drive talking about the hen party and getting slammed in Ibiza."

Brin wrinkled her nose. Torture.

Radd rolled his eyes. "One of them even asked me who did the landscaping at Kagiso?"

"At the lodge?"

Radd shook his head and nodded to the savanna. "Out there."

Brin laughed and shook her head. "Dear God, far too much money and not enough sense."

"Then they had the bright idea of doing a group shot on the edge of the dam. It took me ten minutes to persuade them that the dam was home to a ten-foot crocodile known as Big Daddy."

"Is that true?" Brin asked.

"No, but there is a resident pod of hippos in the dam who don't like being disturbed."

"And hippos kill a lot of people in Africa," Brin replied.

Radd sent her an admiring glance, his dark eyes warm. "You've been reading up."

Brin shrugged, knowing that her cheeks were probably pink from his praise. "I love it here, I'm fascinated. Though it would be amazing to be here without…"

Brin stop speaking, not wanting to say anything negative about his guests. Radd finished her sentence for her. "Without the wedding party? Not your type of people?"

Not at all. "I'm sure they are very nice when you get to know them," Brin diplomatically replied.

"But you wouldn't bet your life on it," Radd told her, laughing. "Honey, your lips say one thing, but your eyes tell the truth. They aren't windows to your soul, they are six-foot-high billboards. And, even if I couldn't read your eyes, your total avoidance of the wedding party would be a damn big clue that you don't like them. Why, is it because they are rich?"

"I'm not that shallow," Brin replied, not happy that he could read her so well.

"No, you're not. Neither are you a snob or

quick to judge, so I'm curious as to why you have made up your mind about Naledi and company so quickly. In fact, even before they arrived..."

Brin heard the knock on the door and thanked God and all his angels and archangels for the distraction. Someone above was looking after her because Radd's questions were coming a little too close for comfort. Radd stood up and walked into the villa, and Brin released a relieved sigh. She heard his low murmur of thanks and he soon returned holding a tray, which he placed on the table between them. A full carafe of coffee, a huge bowl of fruit salad, fresh croissants and fig jam. But, instead of resuming his seat, Radd pulled off his shirt and Brin sucked in her breath at his broad chest, lightly covered with hair, his ridged stomach, the hint of hip muscles sliding beneath the band of his shorts.

He stood with his back to her, looking past the water hole to the savanna beyond, and Brin looked her fill, taking in the way the early morning sunlight bounced off his dark hair. She longed to run her hands over his broad shoulders, kiss the bumps of his spine and discover whether his butt was really as firm as it looked. She wanted to take a bite out of his thick biceps, feel if the hair on his legs was as crisp as she imagined.

He'd been a perfect gentleman and, honestly, she was over it. She wanted to enjoy that amazing outdoor shower, share that slipper bath, drop into that plunge pool naked... with him.

She wanted his mouth on hers, his hands skating over her body, her thighs parting...

As if he could hear her thoughts, Radd turned and his eyes slammed into hers. His hands, gripping the railing behind him, turned white and, as a band of heat warmed her from the inside out, she felt her nipples contract.

Radd's eyes dropped to her chest and before her eyes, she saw him swell, his erection tenting the fabric of his cotton shorts.

He wanted her.

She wanted him.

But Radd didn't move. His eyes just burned and a muscle in his cheek danced. "If I kiss you, there's no going back, Brinley," Radd growled the words, his low tone saturated with emotion.

Brin swallowed and nodded.

"Say the words, Brinley. Know what you are asking."

Brinley gathered her courage and forced her brain to form the words, to verbalize what she wanted. He was right, there was no going back from this.

"I want you, I'd like...you know." Brin floundered, heat flooding her face. But she wouldn't look away, she refused to feel embarrassed about wanting Radd. She was an adult, unattached, and so was he. They were allowed to do this.

Radd momentarily lifted his hands to cup her face in his hands. "God, you are beautiful."

Brin stared into his eyes as she waited for him to kiss her, enjoying this moment of delayed gratification.

Radd seemed equally happy to draw out the moment, leaning over her but not yet touching her. He simply stared at her and, when the moment became too intense, gratification too difficult to ignore, Brin lifted her hand to touch his jaw, heavy with stubble. Her thumb drifted over his bottom lip.

"Kiss me, Radd."

Was that her voice, sultry and sexy? It had to be, because Radd's lips curved into a smile and he lowered his head, whispering his response.

"Gladly."

His kiss, long-awaited, was heat and heaven, both decadent and divine. Radd kept his hands on her cheeks, the only contact they had apart from their mouths, knowing that this was enough, right now. In a few minutes, they'd want more but for now, this sweet and sexy exchange was both reassuring and ridiculously raunchy.

At the same time Radd's tongue slipped past her teeth to slide against hers, he easily pulled her to her feet and against his chest. His erection pushed into her stomach and one hand rested on her bottom, acquainting himself with her shape. His other hand skimmed up her side and came to rest on her breast, his thumb sliding across her tight nipple.

Her thoughts hazy, her mind and body focused on what he was doing to her—his lips on her nipple through the material of her vest had her whimpering with delight—and the way her hands skimmed over his body. It took Brin a few moments to realize that the banging she could hear was not her heart but an insistent rap on the door to the villa.

Pulling back, she pulled a strand of her hair from Radd's stubble and cocked her head.

"Come back here," Radd growled, his hand encircling her neck to pull her mouth back to his.

Brin sank back into his kiss, but another hard rap on the door fractured the moment. Radd cursed but his eyes didn't leave hers. "Ignore it," he told her.

"Radd!"

Yep, that was Naledi's voice and she didn't sound happy. Brin stared at Radd and watched as irritation and frustration jumped into his eyes. "What the hell does she want now?"

Another rap, harder this time, told them that she wasn't going away.

"I swear to God I'm going to kill her. And then I will fire the staff member who escorted her down here."

Brin winced at his hard, cold tone and

stepped away from him, immediately feeling cold and exposed, and more than a little vulnerable. The moment had been so perfect, would they ever be able to re-create it? Would she ever be this brave again? She wasn't sure.

Radd saw something on her face, because his expression softened and he bent down to skim his lips across hers. "Don't retreat, Brin. Let me just deal with this and I'll be back, okay?"

Radd waited, his deep blue eyes nearly black with need, looking for reassurance that she wouldn't change her mind, that they'd be able to pick up where they left off. She wanted to tell him that they would, but she wasn't sure; Brin didn't know if she could be brave twice.

And Radd knew it.

"One step forward, ten back," Radd muttered, his frustration evident in his snappy sentence.

Another rap on the door resulted in Radd snapping out a harsh "Relax, for God's sake, I'm coming!"

Brin watched as he picked up his shirt and dragged it over his head, his eyes blazing with annoyance and his thinned lips reflecting his displeasure. Brin was glad that she wasn't on the other side of the door, she didn't want to be on the receiving end of his anger.

Brin heard the outside door open and, although she couldn't see the door, and their unwelcome visitors couldn't see into the room, she could still hear the exchange.

"Naledi." Radd's greeting was polite, but anyone with a brain in their head would recognize the annoyance in his voice. "How can I help you?"

"I need an extra room, the bridesmaids sharing the Serengeti have had an argument and need some space, and I understand that you have another villa that is available," Naledi replied. "I need them separated."

"Mari, I assume that you explained to Ms. Radebe that wouldn't be possible?" Radd asked.

"I did."

Brin smiled at Mari's tart response and hoped that the Radebes would leave the staff an enormous tip when they left on Friday. If they didn't, and Brin wasn't convinced they would, she hoped Radd rewarded them for not killing their demanding guests.

"Her job is to cater to our every whim and I do not understand why I am standing here and nothing is happening. She's not a very good manager, and I think you should fire her."

Brin's eyes widened. Okay, there was no way that Radd would stand for that type of talk. Not only was Mari exceptional at her job, but she and Radd had been friends since they were kids. He'd jump to her defense, any minute now.

Brin waited, and then waited some more. When Radd didn't defend Mari, her heart dropped to her toes. She knew how it felt to be falsely accused, to be blamed for something that wasn't her fault. She'd endured Kerry's unreasonable anger on too many occasions to count and she'd prayed, wished, her mom would stand up for her, just once.

But that never happened.

Even Kerry's making out with her boyfriend had been swept under the rug, dismissed. Her wants, needs or feelings meant nothing. Like

Naledi, keeping Kerry happy was all that was important, no matter who it hurt.

Brin mentally begged Radd to stand up to the witch!

"I'm sorry you think that, Naledi."

What? That was it? Come on, Radd, do better!

"The food is mediocre, the service second rate and I'm really not happy with the flowers."

What? Radd told her she'd loved the flowers when she'd arrived! And how dare she criticize Mari's staff when they'd been run off their feet with ridiculous requests. And the food was divine!

"I'm afraid it's not possible for anyone move into the spare villa, Naledi, it's privately owned and isn't part of the lodge," Radd said.

"Well, call the owner and get permission!" Naledi retorted. "Come on, chop, chop!"

Brin felt her temper catch alight. Man, she sounded just like Kerry. What, did these socialites and influencers all go to bitch school?

"It wasn't a suggestion, Radd, I need an extra room. And you, Mari—is that your name?—get your act together. And tell your staff to do the same. I do not want to have another conversation about your lack of attentiveness again."

Radd would say something now, of course he would. He wouldn't let her revolting attitude go unchallenged. When neither Radd nor Mari defended each other or themselves, Brin decided she'd heard enough.

Stomping across the room, she stepped into the narrow hallway and took in the scene before her. Radd stood statue-still, his face a cold, hard mask and Mari's eyes held the fine sheen of tears.

Naledi, dressed in a pair of skin-tight shorts and a tiny top, looked like she was enjoying herself immensely. *It is dangerous,* Brin thought, *but someone has to say something.* Then, *This isn't your fight, retreat now and keep the peace.*

She wanted to, and Brin felt herself take a step back, the tension making her throat close. How many times had she been in Mari's position, desperate for someone to be the voice of reason? To stand up for her, to stand up for what was right?

It would be easy to walk away, she'd done it a hundred, five hundred, times before. Walking away was what she did. And did well.

So walk away then…

She wanted to, she did, but her feet refused to obey her brain's command. *You're not really going to insert yourself into this fight, are you, Brin? It's not your problem and you don't handle confrontation well. You can't, at the best of times, stick up for yourself, remember?*

But she could try, just this once, stick up for Mari and her staff and restore a little balance.

"Good morning, Naledi." She, at least, could aim for a modicum of politeness.

Naledi gave her an up-and-down, not-worth-my-notice look. The last of Brin's hesitation fled and her only thought was…*oh, game on.*

"Did you dump an extra dose of bitch tonic in your coffee this morning, Miss Radebe?" Brin asked her, making sure her voice was loaded with disdain.

"Excuse me?" Naledi spluttered.

"You are acting like a spoiled child," Brin told her, keeping her tone low. She knew, from dealing with her sister, that cutting sentences quietly stated had far more of an effect than loud accusations.

"Brinley, stay out of this," Radd told her, his voice as hard as granite.

Not a chance. Not now that she'd begun, anyway. She ignored Radd's order and held Naledi's dark, dismissive eyes. "Mari and her staff are wonderful and incredibly talented, and you know it. They deserve an apology and, better yet, to be treated like human beings and not your personal slaves. Furthermore..."

"Brinley, enough!"

"Too late, Radd. If you won't stick up for them then I will!" Brin told him, furious at his lack of support for his people. "I know how Mari and her people feel, it's deeply frustrating trying to please people who refuse to be pleased."

Brin's temper was slow to erupt but unstoppable when it did, and she was fast losing control of it. The combination of having her morning of passion interrupted—would that ever happen again?—her disappointment in Radd for not sticking up for his people, and feeling like she'd rolled back six months and was dealing with her sister again was a volatile combination.

Hauling in some air, she sent Naledi a scathing look. "God, if your fans could see you now. You're acting like an entitled, spoiled, complete witch. And here's a fun fact, the world does not revolve around you."

Brin, shaking with anger, jammed her index finger into Radd's bicep. "Seriously, if you cave and open up that private residence, I swear I will never talk to you again."

"Are you going to let her talk to me like that?" Naledi screamed at Radd. "Who does she think she is?"

Brin caught Mari's eye and she lifted her chin in a quick movement that neither Radd nor Naledi caught. But Brin understood her silent message: *Thanks for the support but enough. Now, retreat.*

It was a good plan. Because if she stayed she might be tempted to scratch Naledi's eyes out.

"Let's all calm down, shall we?" Radd said, his voice perfectly cool and even. "Mari, escort Miss Radebe back to her room. Can you send a bottle of champagne, our best vintage, and have the staff squeeze some fresh orange juice for mimosas? And maybe a basket of croissants? I'll catch up in a few minutes."

"Of course," Mari replied.

Brin felt Radd's hands on her waist and she yelped as he easily lifted her and walked her backward into his villa. He kicked the door closed with his foot and backed her up against the wall. Brin looked up into his furious face and dismissed her fear. Radd would not hurt her, physically.

Emotionally, he could rip her apart.

"How dare you interfere in a situation that has nothing to do with you? You have no idea what you are risking!" Radd demanded, his voice coated in anger and disdain. "This is *my* property, *my* business, *my* guests, *my* staff. You are…"

She waited for the "nothing," the "you're not important," but the phrases never left his lips. Instead they hung between them, loud and tangible.

Radd's hands dropped from her shoulders and he shook his head, frustration rolling off his body in waves. "Don't confuse my attraction to you with me giving you permission to meddle in my life, Brinley Riddell. Because that will never, ever happen. Understood?"

Radd waited for her nod before dropping his hands and leaving her, slumped against the wall.

Radd wasn't a fool, he'd seen the disdain in Brin's eyes hours earlier when he didn't defend Mari or his staff. But worse than that was seeing her respect for him fade.

Radd, walking back along the wooden path toward his villa, jammed his hands into the pockets of his shorts, convinced that his head was about to split apart.

Five days ago, if someone had dared to interfere with his business, his decisions or his life, he would've, without hesitation, told them off and immediately broken off their liaison. Thanks to having a reputation of being cold as ice and unemotional, nobody, ever, questioned him. Few people had the strength or the guts, but Brin had simply waded into a battle that wasn't hers to wage.

He was both frustrated and proud of her.

Radd rubbed his hands over his face, irked.

Before she dropped into his life, his emotions were tamped down, buttoned-up, kept corralled and constrained. Brin, somehow and strangely, held the key to unlock a myriad of unwanted and unneeded emotions.

But she didn't know, and he couldn't explain, that he was caught between doing what was *right*—yes, he should've defended his staff—and what was *needed*, which was keeping the Radebes happy until the sale agreement for the mine was finalized.

Was the mine and the PR campaign worth it? In a few months, it would be the second anniversary of his parents' deaths. Yeah, sure, some upper-echelon businessmen were still pissed at his father, at deals that went south, money that was lost. But, Jesus, that happened more than twenty years ago...

Did his actions still reflect on him and Digby? Was buying the mine, being manipulated by Vincent, hosting this damn week and the wedding worth all the crap and stress he was dealing with?

For the first time in, well, forever, Radd wasn't sure whether it was. And, God this hurt to admit, was their stupidly expensive

PR and marketing campaign just a way to boost his ego, an expensive way to show the world that you *could* get oranges from apple trees?

Would anyone, apart from him and Digby, and the workers at the mine, even care whether there was a new school, better working conditions, an increase in salaries?

Shouldn't that be the norm, not the exception?

Radd rubbed his hands over his face, feeling utterly exhausted. And he still had to deal with Brin, who probably thought he was a weak fool. But she had no idea how much control he'd needed not to tell the spoiled socialite exactly what he thought of her and her asinine demands. That was why he had remained quiet, he'd been trying to control his own temper. Brin hadn't held back and, while he did wish she hadn't jumped into the fray, he couldn't help but admire her for doing so.

Brinley, Radd was starting to believe, was a good person to have in your corner. But he knew that he'd lost that chance…

God, what a mess.

Radd walked into his villa and nodded to

the housekeeper, who was smoothing down the cover of his enormous bed.

"Hey, Greta."

"Mr. Radd." Greta smiled at him as she carefully placed a pillow in the center of the bed. "I'll just gather the dirty towels and get out of your way."

"No hurry," Radd told her, moving into the living area. Walking over to the always-open doors leading to his deck, he gripped the top of the frame and looked toward the plunge pool. Brin stood in the clear water, her slim back to him, looking through the rails of the balcony to the water hole below.

A couple of buffalo cows stood at the water's edge and Radd scanned behind them, instantly picking out the rest of the herd standing in the dense bush. In the far distance, a giraffe and her calf ambled across an open patch of savanna. Not knowing how to break the tension between them—he knew that she was aware of his presence—he looked up at the sky, which was that perfect shade of African blue, so thick and heavy he could shove his hand through it.

Radd tried to break the heavy silence. "Let's clear the air, Brinley."

Brin didn't pull her eyes off the water hole. Right, the silent treatment.

Excellent.

Radd dropped his arms, pulled his phone out of his pocket and placed it on the nearest table. Kicking off his flip-flops, he whipped off his shirt and walked over to the plunge pool, dropping into the heated water behind her.

Damn, the water felt good. The best thing—apart from feeling Brin in his arms—that had happened to him this morning. Pushing his wet hair off his face, Radd joined Brin at the side of the pool, his arms brushing hers, and she immediately pulled away and put six inches between them.

Yeah, getting back in her good graces wasn't going to be easy.

Radd sighed, wondering why it felt so imperative for him to do so. She'd just walked into his life and in a few days she would be out of it, so why did he care so much about what she thought of him? He didn't give a damn about how people viewed him, well, except for Digby and a handful of old, good friends. Women, let's face it, were easy.

But Brin wasn't. Easy, that is, nor was she run-of-the-mill.

She had a backbone he hadn't expected, a fierce temper when roused by injustice. And complete disdain for anyone who used their position and power to intimidate.

He liked that. Hell, he liked her. More than he'd like anyone for a long, long time. And that was very bad news indeed. She had the power, damn her, to be the catalyst for him to change. He didn't want to change, he liked his life the way it was.

"I sent lunch but was told that you didn't eat either," Radd commented.

"I'm sorry to have wasted the food, but I wasn't hungry."

Hell, he didn't care about two plates of food; he wanted to know what was going on in her head. Brin reached for her sunglasses and slid them onto her face, covering her beautiful eyes. Like her conservative, full-piece swimsuit, her lack of eye contact was another barrier to regaining the easy, laidback companionship they'd shared before.

And it had been easy; he enjoyed having her in his space and appreciated the fact that she didn't need to be entertained. In the time they spent together alone, he felt completely comfortable reading a report or working while she read or dozed. And when they did talk, their conversation flowed. She had a self-deprecating sense of humor he enjoyed, and he found himself laughing at her wry observations. Her love for Kagiso was obvious, and she seemed eager to hear about his life on this farm as a child and tales of his wild Tempest-Vane ancestors, most of whom were eccentric. A few were certifiably nuts.

They'd been comfortable, relaxed and, dare he say it, happy.

Until the ugly scene this morning.

Radd opened his mouth to try to breach the distance between them, but Brin whipping her glasses off her face and tossing them onto the deck had his mouth snapping closed. When her eyes slammed into his, he saw her anger and, wait, was that embarrassment?

"I'm am very sorry I interfered this morning. You're right, it had nothing to do with me and I shouldn't have said anything. I'm

sorry if I put you in an uncomfortable position." Brin hauled in a breath and managed,
just, to meet his eyes. "I didn't like the way
Naledi spoke to Mari and I was upset that
you didn't stand up for Mari, for your staff.
But you were right, it had absolutely nothing
to do with me."

Radd could tell, despite being a man and
generally clueless, that she was still properly,
deeply upset. He rubbed his stubble-covered
jaw, trying to make sense of her extreme reaction. Yes, she and Mari seemed to like each
other, but they weren't best friends, so why
was she so intent on defending her and his
staff?

Making a concerted effort to keep his voice
low and nonaccusatory—he was trying to understand, not start another fight—he asked
for more of an explanation.

Brin hesitated before throwing her hands
in the air. "You are part of their social group,
a member of their elite club! You're as powerful as them, certainly as rich! You should
protect and defend those weaker than you,
the people you employ!" Brin hauled herself

out of the pool in a fluid movement, all long legs and feminine grace.

And damn, she was even more beautiful when she was furious. Radd couldn't resist looking at her firm, high breasts. In the pool, against his shorts, parts of him were rising, too.

Not that she'd appreciate his response...

Brin's eyes dropped down and widened when she saw his evident need for her. She threw up her hands and scowled at him. "Really?"

He shrugged. "I'm a guy, you're wearing next to nothing, and I can't help thinking about what we were doing when we were interrupted earlier."

Brin stomped over to a lounger, snatched up her towel and wrapped it around her torso, hiding her curvy body. Damn.

Radd blew air into his cheeks and pulled himself out of the pool. He walked across the deck to where she stood, water running off him and darkening the planks of the light wooden floor.

"I wasn't meaning to make light of your

anger, but you're an incredibly sexy woman, a woman I want."

"That ship has sailed."

"I gathered that." Radd folded his arms across his chest and looked for words to regain some lost ground, preferably without having to explain why keeping the Radebes happy was so very important to him. She knew the basics, the surface stuff, but he couldn't find the words to explain the PR campaign, rebranding their name, putting his parent's ugly legacy to rest. Rebuilding a legacy they could be proud of...

"I need to keep the Radebes happy. Can we leave it at that?"

"At the risk of alienating your staff, losing their respect? My respect?" Brin's words were as hard and cold as an Arctic wind. "Oh, but wait, our opinions don't matter, because we're not as rich or as powerful or as successful as you."

"I didn't say that!" Radd snapped back, stung.

"But it was what you meant!"

"The hell it was!"

A tide of red crept up Brin's neck and he

could see the light of battle in her eyes. Radd knew that he was in for another tongue lashing. He wasn't wrong. And that was okay, he far preferred angry Brin to the subservient creature who'd apologized earlier.

"I know your type. Hell, I worked for people like you, Radd! I was blamed and castigated for things I didn't do, things that weren't my fault and over which I had no control! People like you, like my…like Naledi are entitled and demanding and disrespectful, and why the hell am I arguing with you about this?" Brin pushed her fingers into her hair, pushing away the long, wet curls. "This is ridiculous! Just get me out of here! Take me back to Cape Town!"

Oh, hell no. "Running away, Brin?"

"Just removing myself from your company," Brin replied, turning around and walking into the room. Radd watched her go and, when she stopped suddenly, he looked past her to see Mari standing by the doorway, looking uncomfortable.

"Sorry, I knocked."

His villa was like Grand Central Station today. If another person arrived uninvited, he just might lose it. Radd pulled in a deep breath, then another and tried to hold on to his temper.

"What is it?"

Mari sent him a *Don't mess with me* look. Another female who was mad at him. Wonderful. "I had Simon bring a vehicle over and Chef has packed a basket of food for your dinner and breakfast."

Mari turned her attention to Brin, sending her a sweet smile. "Thank you for sticking up for us, Brin, but it wasn't necessary. We've had worse guests than the Radebe party and we know how to handle them. Mostly it's best if you just let them rant and vent and then do what you intended to do all along. Radd knows this, as do I."

Brin rolled her eyes at Mari's calm statement.

Mari turned her attention back to Radd. "I think you and Brin need a break, and it would be sensible to put some distance between Brin and Naledi right now. She's still demanding an apology from you, Brin."

Radd's "that's not going to happen" coincided with Brin's "I'd rather die."

Mari rubbed her forehead with the tips of her fingers before refocusing her attention back on the pair of them. She was acting as if they were both high-maintenance toddlers. "Guys, that wasn't a suggestion. And I think we could all do with a break."

"I think Cape Town is far enough away," Brin said, her expression stubborn.

"Let's not get carried away, honey," Mari said on a small smile. She turned to Radd. "Take Brin to The Treehouse, Radd. Leave now, while the Radebes are having their afternoon siesta. Your vehicle is parked by the staff quarters and you can avoid the lodge altogether."

Radd nodded, thinking that Mari's suggestion held a lot of merit. Maybe if he and Brin were alone, truly alone, they could recapture some of their earlier ease. And, even if they didn't, they'd give Naledi time to calm the hell down.

And it had been a while since he'd been to The Treehouse.

Pulling a towel out of the pile on the shelf near the door, he swiped the cloth over his chest and rubbed his hair. Mari sent him a

Get this done look and he gave her a small nod, hoping he could get Brin to agree.

How to do that?

He thought it best to stick to the facts and hopefully, whet her curiosity. "The Tree-house is a secure, completely private and lav-ish platform above massive boulders. Behind the structure is woodlands, and it's my favor-ite place for watching the sun rise and set."

Brin's eyes narrowed. "How many beds?"

He couldn't lie. "One. But it's a huge bed and the same rules apply there as here. You've got to ask…"

"Yeah, that didn't work out so well this morning."

"It would've worked out fine if we hadn't been interrupted," Radd muttered, still feel-ing resentful. He now had to work ten times harder to get back to that place they had been, and Radd wasn't sure if they would get there.

The thought depressed him. And the fact that he could feel depressed, depressed him more.

God, he was losing it.

Radd, irritated with himself and with Brin for not making this situation easier, found his patience slipping. "I'm going to The Tree-house. Come if you want to. If you don't, fine."

Brin took her time making up her mind and Radd forced himself not to display his impatience. This slip of a girl didn't need to know how much she rattled him. And how much he hoped she said yes.

"Does this place have a shower?"

"Solar-powered."

Radd sent Mari a *Help me* look, and she rolled her eyes before speaking. "If the lodge is a six-star establishment, then The Tree-house is a notch above. It's a pretty special place, Brin, and you'll regret not seeing it. It will be worth putting up with his company, I promise you."

Thanks, Mari, Radd thought, narrowing his eyes at his old friend.

"Fine," Brin muttered, stomping inside.

Mari smiled at him. "Prepared to do some groveling, Tempest-Vane?"

The hell he was! He was alpha to his core, groveling wasn't part of his vocabulary. God, he wasn't even good at apologizing! Mari's eyebrows rose higher at his silence and he finally gave in, his shoulders slumping. "I might have to do a little damage control," he reluctantly admitted.

Mari patted his shoulder. "Try not to hurt yourself trying something new, my friend."

Ha-ha, Radd thought, glaring at her departing back.

CHAPTER EIGHT

WHAT WAS SHE doing in this vehicle? Why hadn't she stayed in Radd's villa and given them both some time apart and space to cool down?

Brinley pushed her sunglasses up into her hair and shook her head at her behavior. While she didn't believe she had been completely in the wrong to defend Mari, she shouldn't have jumped feet first into Radd's business. And Mari, smart and independent, didn't seem the type to need defending. But Naledi just pushed every button Brinley had...

And what had she been thinking, allowing her fight with Radd to reignite after she finally had found the courage to apologize? And what was she doing here? Was she just a glutton for punishment?

But the heart of the matter was that, despite the fact she was still irritated with Radd, she didn't want to miss out on one moment she could be with him. She would leave his life the day after tomorrow and, annoyingly, wherever he was, was where she wanted to be.

He was arrogant and irritating and implacable and annoying and sexy and...

Brin shook her head and noticed that Radd was finally, after an hour of driving in silence, slowing down. He braked and switched off the ignition.

"We're here."

All she could see was rocks. Confused, Brinley exited the vehicle at the base of a massive set of boulders towering above her. Pulling her overnight bag over her shoulder, she followed Radd as he stepped onto a walkway made of anchored wooden planks climbing in a zigzag pattern up the rocks. Radd easily carried a huge picnic basket and his own small rucksack. A two-way radio was tucked into the back pocket of his cargo shorts and he had a rifle slung over his shoulder.

Brin turned the corner and looked across the walkway spanning two boulders, and her mouth dropped open. To the left was a rolling carpet of open savanna, dotted by the occasional tree. To the right were more boulders, some of which had tree roots clinging to their mottled surface. Stopping, she pushed her fist into her sternum and looked at the structure in front of her, sophisticated and simple.

At its core, The Treehouse was a wooden deck, encircled with a wire-and-wood railing, thirty feet off the ground. A reed roof covered half of the area and beneath it was an enormous bed dressed in white linen, piled high with pillows and surrounded by a heavy mosquito net, sumptuous and sexy and sensual.

A small table sat in one corner of the deck overlooking the rolling savanna. In the other corner sat a pile of thick, huge cushions, suitable for a sultan's tent. Numerous old-fashioned lamps were placed at strategic intervals along the outside of the deck, providing light when night fell.

Man, it was romantic. All that was missing was an icy bottle of champagne in a silver bucket and blood-red rose petals.

Brin followed Radd across the walkway onto the main deck and watched as he set the picnic basket down next to the small table. He tossed his rucksack in the general direction of the bed and gripped the railing, shoving his sunglasses onto the top of his head. He scanned the bushveld, and Brin saw the tension ease in his shoulders and the hard line of his jaw soften.

He loved every inch of Kagiso, but this place obviously held a special place in his heart.

Brin dropped her bag onto the bench seat at the end of the bed and, slipping out of her shoes, walked barefoot across the smooth planks to peek behind the screen that formed the headboard of the bed. Her breath hitched again with delight; she'd expected rustic and basic, yet the bathroom was anything but. Instead of a shower, an antique cast-iron slipper bath took pride of place in the center of the space and his and hers sinks covered a reed wall. Pulling open a door made from reeds, she smiled at the private toilet, one of her biggest worries about sleeping in the bush alleviated.

Brin left the bathroom area and walked back toward Radd. By now it was late afternoon and, with the setting sun, the temperature had dropped, too. Rubbing her arms, she sank to sit cross-legged on one of the huge cushions, her eyes bouncing over the incredible landscape.

An eland bull drifted across the savanna and a warthog scampered past him. With the sun setting, the light turned ethereal and magical, a time for fairies and pixies, pure enchantment.

Pity she and Radd weren't currently talking.

She'd expected him to tear strips off her for being rude to Naledi. She kept waiting for the hammer to fall, for him to say something about her behavior, to castigate her for injecting herself into a situation that had nothing to do with her. But hours had passed and he'd said nothing and, maybe, he didn't intend to.

Why? Was he trying to lull her into a false sense of complacency? When she relaxed, would he rant and rave? It was a favorite tactic of Kerry's, which she'd learned at their mom's knee.

"Will you please just tell me that I was out

of line earlier so that we can move on?" Brin demanded, frustrated.

Radd handed her a small frown. "But you weren't wrong, I was," Radd said, balancing on his haunches as he inspected the picnic basket. He rested his arm on his thigh as he looked at her. "You were right earlier, Naledi was being a class-A bitch. But I can't afford to piss her, or her father, off. But, you'll be happy to know, I did apologize to Mari, and promised her and the staff a massive bonus when the Radebe party leaves."

Brin's eyes widened at his admission. Really? Wow. For the first time, her angry outburst hadn't been met with derision or payback, sarcasm or delayed mental punishment.

Annoyance crossed Radd's face, but Brin sensed it wasn't directed at her. "Vincent Radebe now owns what used to be a Tempest-Vane mine, one of the most productive diamond mines in the world," Radd said as he stood up, two crystal glasses and a bottle of red wine in his hand. "Over the past ten years, Digby and I have made it a mission to purchase back all the companies that our father inherited and then discarded, including The Vane, Kagiso and other properties and businesses."

"Did you have to buy back the family home and vineyard?" Brin asked, curious.

Radd shook his head. "That was in a separate trust, and my parents couldn't sell it. It's handed down through the generations from oldest son to oldest son."

"Wow, your ancestors didn't much value girls, did they?"

"Sadly, no."

Brin hadn't expected him to talk and definitely hadn't expected him to open up. Not wanting to stem the flow of words, she wrapped her arms around her bent knees and waited for more. When he didn't speak, she rolled her finger in the air. "You were talking about Vincent…"

"Yeah. Vincent's a canny operator. He quickly sussed out how much we want the mine and made us jump through hoops to get it. He also made us pay over the odds and jerked us around because he lost a pile of money on a deal my father screwed up.

"The mine is productive, well run and profitable, and he wanted to exact a little revenge on Gil through us. We had to work so damn hard to get him to consider selling." Radd dropped down to sit on the cushion opposite her, his navy eyes frustrated. He glanced from her to the picnic basket and waved his glass in its direction. "If you are hungry, there's hummus and red pepper dip and crackers. We're having a cold lobster, crab and prawn salad and crusty bread for dinner, followed by handmade Belgian chocolates."

It sounded delicious, but she was hungry for conversation, for an explanation.

Radd sipped his wine before setting it down next to his cushion and draping his forearms over his bended knees. She could barely remember the well-dressed man in the designer clothes she'd met on that beachfront in Camps Bay, the one driving a super expensive car and looking like a modern-day hero billionaire. This Radd, dressed in an expensive but lightweight cotton shirt and expensive cargo shorts, looked far more disreputable and, in a strange way, more human.

More approachable.

"Vincent tied the purchase of the mine to

certain favors he knew I could grant him," Radd explained. "Naledi is his only daughter and she has him firmly wrapped around her little finger. She wanted the biggest, shiniest, brightest, most noteworthy wedding in the country and that meant having it at The Vane. Her wedding at The Vane and a week at Kagiso for the wedding party were sweeteners I had to throw in before Vincent would start negotiations to sell the mine."

Ah, now his pandering to those impossible people made sense. Brin swallowed some more wine before resting the foot of her glass on her knee. "So, when this is over, you'll own the mine?"

Radd nodded. He looked down at his feet, then past her shoulder and then back to his feet. Brin tipped her head to the side, wondering why he was avoiding her gaze.

"There's something else you're not telling me. I mean, you don't have to but…"

He took a long time to answer and, for a minute, Brin didn't think he would. "When we have the mine, we are going to launch a massive PR campaign and rebranding exercise to, hopefully, rehabilitate the family name."

"Because of your parents?"

Radd nodded. "Their reputation is like a bad smell that won't go away." He stared down at the wine in his glass, his expression thoughtful. "Dig and I have worked so damn hard and there are things we want to do, projects we want to explore, but we can't do *everything* alone. And certain business people won't touch us because there's a belief that we are as dishonest as our father, as out of control as both our parents."

"And you think a PR campaign will change that?" Brin asked.

"Maybe not. But it's worth a shot. I also intend on giving some personal interviews explaining our rationale, highlighting our commitment to good governance and community involvement. Make it clear that we are tough negotiators but fair, and that we say what we mean and mean what we say."

Brin couldn't imagine what living with his parents had been like, but it was obvious it had damaged Radd to an extent. She wasn't sure his expensive campaign would change anything, though. She'd begged her sister and mother to change, but nothing she said could sway them. "Sometimes people believe what they believe and always will, Radd. Some minds will never be changed."

"But I still feel the need to try. I need to do it for Jack, for my grandfather, the grandfathers that came before him. They were good men."

"That's a lot of pressure from dead people," Brin pointed out.

"What do you mean?"

Brin shrugged. "I think that if you had to have a conversation with Jack and your grandfather, with all the grandfathers, I'm pretty sure they'd tell you to stop thinking so much and be happy. To stop worrying so much about what people think about you and start living life, on your terms."

Radd looked like she'd slapped him, and Brin cursed her tongue. She waved her words away. "But hell, what do I know? I ran away from a bossy sister and an impossible-to-please mother."

They'd both been hurt by family, sliced and

diced by the people who were supposed to love them the most.

"Families can be…" Brin tested the words on her tongue… *Infuriating*? *Annoying*? *Hurtful*? *Soul-destroying*? She settled for "…complicated."

Radd's mouth briefly curled at her understatement. "Tell me about yours. You've given me a little information, but you know far more about me than I do about you."

Brin jerked and hoped he didn't notice. And what could she say, what should she say about her equally messed-up situation? "What do you want to know?" she hedged, desperately racking her mind for a way to distract him.

"Whatever you want to tell me," Radd commented, stretching out his legs and leaning back on his hands. "What do your parents do? Your sister?"

"As I mentioned, my mother raised me as a single mom, then she met and married my stepfather, who is an accountant, and they had another child, my younger sister. I've never met my real dad. My mom helps my sister run her business." There, that was subtle, but still vague.

"In?" Radd persisted.

Ah, damn his curiosity. "Public relations."

Well, being a celebrity, an influencer and sometimes an actor could be called PR, couldn't it?

"You're even more reticent than I am," Radd complained, tipping his head back as Brin climbed to her feet.

Maybe so, but she couldn't tell him that her sister was Naledi's archrival, that if her presence was discovered here, she'd put his plans in jeopardy. No, he most definitely did not need to know that… He'd told her he didn't like secrets, and she was keeping a whopper to herself.

Radd rolled to his feet and came to stand beside her at the railing. Brin could feel his heat, and his sex and sunshine scent made her feel weak at the knees.

"When you went off at me earlier, it sounded like you've had experience being treated badly. Have you?"

Brin chose her words carefully. She wanted to tell him, she *did*, but she didn't want to risk him being angry with her and spoiling the evening. She would tell him, she should, but not now. "My previous boss was difficult. And entitled. Honestly, I was, *am*, surprised I said anything. Normally I keep quiet and accept that status quo."

"Really? What's different about me?"

Because you make me feel like I am standing in a safe zone, a solid barrier between me and the world. Because I feel you might be the one person who gets me. But, while we might be walking this section of the road together, soon our paths will diverge.

"I guess it's because you're not going to be a permanent part of my life."

Brin thought she saw a flicker of hurt in Radd's eyes at her off-the-cuff comment but immediately dismissed the errant thought. Radd didn't feel enough for her to feel hurt. But there was still a part of her that wanted to reassure him, to tell him that, strangely, she felt comfortable expressing her anger and her disappointment to him. She earlier suspected, but now knew, that Radd would never use her feelings or opinions as a weapon, to dismiss or to diminish her.

He might not agree with her but, around him, Brin never felt less than unimportant.

"So what's your big goal, your life quest?" Radd quietly asked her, loosely holding his glass in his big hand.

Brin hesitated, not wanting to spin more threads that would bind her and Radd together, making it more difficult for her to leave. "I just want to be financially secure and to have my own space to stand in, a spot of sunshine that's mine alone."

"And will you get that once I pay you?"

Brin nodded. "In time. In a few months, I'll own my flower-and-coffee shop and, hopefully, in a few years, I'll be able to buy a house, put a little away for a rainy day."

"Hopefully by then you'll also have buried that death trap you call a car," Radd muttered.

Brin smiled at the note of frustration in his voice. He obviously loved cars and Betsy's lack of well, style, class and running ability offended him. But he didn't understand that upgrading her car would mean taking a loan from her sister or mother, and that would be like walking straight back into the spider's web.

It had taken her far too long to disentangle herself to take that risk.

"I just want to be self-sufficient and independent, Radd." Brin quietly stated. "I don't want to have to answer to anyone ever again. I've spent the last couple of months finding myself."

Radd looked pensive. "I've never really understood that expression. I mean, God, you're not a winning Lotto ticket in a coat pocket."

"But I've felt so lost, like I'm a reflection of Ker...of my mother and sister."

"I think whoever you are, the person you *really* are, is there, deep in you. It's just buried beneath all the crap society feeds us, the messages we received as kids, and what the media tells us we should be. Could finding yourself actually mean returning to yourself, to being the 'you' you were before life and people got their hands on you?"

His words slapped her in her soul, in that place deep down inside that no one ever ventured. Man, he got her, understood her on a deep, dark intrinsic level. Despite not knowing everything about the mixed, complicated relationship between her, her sister and her mother, he managed to nail the proverbial nail on the head.

He understood her in a way she needed to be understood. From the moment she met him, she trusted him… She'd jumped into a plane with him, trusted him to pay her the money she was owed, moved into his villa with him.

Had things turned out differently, she would've trusted him with her body. And she might still do that.

Honesty made her admit she was a probably a hair's breadth from falling in love with him—this man who operated in the same world she'd fought so hard to leave—but trust was far harder to find than love.

And, oh, God, Brin hoped he trusted her, too. Because she thought that maybe he did, just a little, she placed her hand on his arm and waited until he looked up and into her eyes. "That's incredibly profound and I appreciate it more than you know. And because you said that, maybe I can say this…?"

"What?" Radd asked when she hesitated, his expression curious.

"Maybe the PR campaign is necessary, from a business point of view," she shrugged. "Obviously I don't know your business, but I do know that you are nothing like your parents and the people who deal with you are fools if they can't see it. It doesn't matter how people see you, Radd, it's how you see yourself. The only way to stop your parents influencing your life is to stop caring, to accept that they made their own choices and that those choices had nothing to do with you."

Radd stared down at his hands, and Brin didn't push him for a response because their conversation was getting so deep, so intense. *But,* Brin thought as she looked up at the stars, *this is the night, and the place for conversations like these.* She wasn't a fool to think that this was the start of something bright and shiny and new, but she did know that they'd impacted each other, that they'd reshaped each other's thinking.

And that, in itself, was incredibly powerful.

After a delicious dinner, and a conversation filled with laughter, Brin sighed. It was almost a perfect evening, but she wanted more. She wanted a night she'd always remember in crystal clear detail, a wonderful memory to give her comfort when she returned to Cape Town and a Radd-free life.

Because a couple of days did not a relationship make.

But it was one thing to make the mental shift to decide to have sex, but *asking* for one night, a step out of time, was something completely different.

Seriously, Brin thought as she stared at Radd's gorgeous profile in the romantic light of the oil lamps, *why can't he read my mind*? It would be so much easier.

But that was his point, wasn't it? He wanted her to make the first move, to take the initiative because then she could never accuse him of pressuring her. But the fear of rejection, something she'd battled with her entire life, kept the words locked firmly between her teeth. Brin tipped her head back to look at the stars, crystals hanging in a pure black sky. It was so quiet, yet, at the same time, it wasn't. She was used to the sound of vehicles, the hum of their noisy fridge, barking dogs, wind in the tree outside her window. The noise of the bushveld was unlike anything she'd experienced, a dichotomy of silence and noise, both at the same time.

It was the sound of the earth and its creatures sighing, sleeping, dreaming. Even if nothing happened between her and Radd tonight—and she hoped to find the courage soon to ensure it would—it was almost enough just to sit under the low-hanging sky and listen to the sounds of the African night.

She heard the rumble, a displacement of air and, because she happened to be looking at Radd at the time, she saw his attention sharpen, his body tensing.

Brin leaned forward and, needing a connection, placed her hand on his knee. "What? Is everything okay?"

A small smile touched Radd's face and he held up his index finger in a silent request for her to wait. Brin looked around anxiously.

"Shh, relax. Just listen." Radd slid his fingers between hers, gently squeezing. Brin immediately relaxed; he'd protect her, she was safe.

Scooting closer to him, Brin placed her temple on the ball of his shoulder, her thigh aligning with his. Releasing her hand, Radd placed his arm around her back, his hand curving over her hip. His touch felt right and it felt real. If she lifted her head, her mouth would meet his...

A deep sound rumbled through the air, sounding as if it were pulled from the center of the earth and raising the hair on Brin's arms and the back of her neck. It smacked her soul, the deep roar settling in the pockets of her heart and lungs, and twisting her stomach inside out.

"That's a big boy," Radd murmured, his voice lazy.

"Lion?" Brin asked, though she knew it couldn't be anything else.

"Mmm..."

How could he sound so relaxed, like he'd just heard the hooting of an owl or the backfiring of a car? "And he's how close?" Brin demanded, her voice a little shaky.

"A couple of kilometers, at least." Brin felt rather than heard Radd's amusement. "And might I remind you that we are thirty feet in the air, and lions can't jump that high?"

He was laughing at her, but his amusement

wasn't disparaging or patronizing; it was gentle. And kind.

"Feel free to climb into my lap if you feel scared."

It was an offer she couldn't refuse, a chance she had to take. "Okay."

She felt the muscles in his arms and thigh contract, heard his swift intake of breath. Brin wasn't sure how many minutes, or seconds or years, passed, but then Radd's hand touched her jaw, turning and tipping her face up. His eyes were the color of the sky, his scent as earthy and primal as the African night.

"I'm going to ask this once… Are you sure?"

"Very."

And she was. She wanted *one* night, a perfect night. A night with no expectations but only pleasure, hours of hot hands and wet mouths and for them to pretend that they owned the night.

Radd half turned, and Brin felt his hands on her waist, easily lifting her so that she straddled his thighs. She knew that he was trying to be gentle, but gentle didn't suit this environment or what she wanted. She wanted primal, sensual, hot.

Radd's arms tightened around her bottom and lower back. His eyes dropped to her mouth and his fingers tattooed their way up her spine to clasp the back of her head, to pull it down. Without a word, his mouth slanted over hers and his tongue slid past his teeth. A hot ribbon of lust rippled from her mouth to her breasts, to that secret, dark place at the entrance of her womb. Radd pushed his hand up and under her clothes to learn the shape and feel of her breast. Brin whimpered, twisting Radd's linen shirt in her hand. Nothing mattered but his mouth and his hand and the stone-hard length of him pressed between her thighs.

It wasn't supposed to be this wild, this hot, this quickly. She wasn't experienced, true, but this felt bigger, deeper, darker. Brin lifted her fingers to his jaw and nipped, her tongue making tiny forays into his mouth. She felt Radd's hand slide under her top to unhook her bra and then, as his thumbs slid across her nipples, all hell broke loose.

And Brin welcomed the storm.

Their lips collided and Brin, strangely and uncharacteristically, found herself fighting for dominance of the kiss. Radd yanked her lightweight jersey over her head and, without hesitation, grabbed the hem of her button-down shirt and ripped the fabric apart, scattering buttons in every direction and baring her breasts to his mouth. Time stood still and the earth stopped moving as she bore down on his hard erection, desperate to have him inside her, around her.

Radd lifted his head from her chest and his eyes glittered in the moonlight. "You are so incredibly beautiful."

For the first time in her life she felt beautiful, gorgeous, sensual, a goddess being adored by her mate. Unable to speak past the lump in her throat, she pulled his shirt up his chest and over his head, throwing it to the floor.

Brin, needing him and, unable to wait, hopped off Radd and shucked her jeans and panties. Barely giving Radd time to shed his own clothes, she climbed back on him, whimpering when her wet core met his heat and hardness.

Sighing, she tucked her face into his neck and inhaled, desperate to use every sense to experience the essence of making love to him, knowing that she'd need to commit this to memory because it was just one time.

The *only* time.

Brin felt the banked tension in his hand as he gripped her thighs, the urgency in his tongue as he looked for, and found, her mouth. She felt him quiver and knew that, with the slightest provocation, he'd spill himself. Needing more, needing everything, she bore down and clenched her internal muscles.

"Brin, we need a condom. I have some in my toiletry bag."

It took a while for his words to make sense, even longer for her to respond. "I'm on the pill and if you are clean…"

"Physical a couple of months ago. No one since," Radd muttered.

"Well, then…"

Radd touched her, expertly and intimately, and Brin released a cry that was part pleasure, all desire. His fingers lifted her up and up and, when she begged him to come inside her, he entered her in a smooth slide. Brin felt a sob build in her throat; he felt so right, the missing piece of her puzzle.

Riding a hot wave of pure sensation, and wanting to be an active participant in this tsunami-like ride, Brin grabbed his shoulders, swiping her breasts against his chest and seeking his mouth. Brin heard the deep moan in his throat and whimpered as he lifted his hips, burying himself even deeper inside her.

Higher, faster, harder, deeper. Their world receded, and the only question of importance was who was going to come first. Brin whimpered, and Radd shouted as their worlds collided and then exploded. Brin heard his harsh breath in his ear, his hot lips on the cord of her throat. She couldn't tell where he started or she ended, as close as two people could be.

She could stay like this forever, hearts beating in unison, her hands on his back, his holding her hips. She wanted more of this, more of anything he could give her: time, affection, attention.

Love. Love most of all.

Oh, God, no. No, no, no, no, no.

She'd done exactly what she promised herself she wouldn't...

She was so close to falling in love with Radd Tempest-Vane. One more step, a quick slide and she would be there. Brin bit her lip, wondering if she was not confusing great sex with love, an amazing orgasm with affection. She wished she was, because if this was only sex, then walking away would be so much easier. But leaving Radd, carrying on with her life was going to be…well, hard. Different. A little flat and devoid of color.

But she couldn't tell him her feelings, wouldn't let him in on how she felt. Radd insisted on her making the first move to have sex, but Brin wanted him to be the first to breach the subject of feelings and love.

Because while she knew that she was there, or almost there, or something, she had no idea what Radd was thinking or feeling.

And, as she'd learned, people couldn't be forced to give you what you needed, to love you the way you wanted them to….

In the distance, a hyena's mocking laugh pierced the night.

CHAPTER NINE

SEX ISN'T NORMALLY that good, Radd thought as he pulled his vehicle to a stop at the stairs leading up to Kagiso's main reception area. It was a biological function, they were hard-wired as humans to want to procreate and to have fun while they did it.

It wasn't supposed to make your soul jump, your heart settle and your stomach tie itself into a complicated knot.

Radd looked at Brin sitting in the passenger seat next to him. Although she was dressed simply, blue jeans and a white T-shirt, her face free of makeup, and her hair pulled back into a sexy tail, she could rival any super-model. And he should know, since he'd dated a few...

He couldn't wait to take her back to bed.

But sex, great sex, bed-rocking, moon-howling sex, was all they could ever have. He didn't believe in love, commitment or happily-ever-afters; they were a myth, a fairy tale. He wasn't interested in being anyone's husband or significant other.

But if there ever was a woman who could change his mind, Brin would be that person. She was refreshing and without artifice, un-impressed with his wealth, success or looks. She looked past all of that and saw him, saw the man beneath the Tempest-Vane surface. When he was feeling mushy—*vulnerable* was a word he refused to use—he could imagine laying all his fears, and dreams, at her feet, knowing that she wouldn't trample on either.

But that was impossible; he wouldn't see her again after he delivered her to her house tomorrow. He'd kiss her goodbye and walk away and return to the real world. In time, he'd start thinking of her as just another pass-ing ship in the night.

But the thought of never seeing her again sent his stomach plunging to his toes, quickly followed by waves of anger and frustration. He shouldn't be thinking like this, shouldn't be allowing his thoughts to drift in that di-rection.

And God, he couldn't help wondering if

any of their deep conversations would be repeated, if what he shared would end up in the public domain. He didn't think they would, but that familiar dread, so adept at twisting his innards in knots, settled down and made itself comfortable. He knew better than to let his mouth run, if he'd kept his thoughts to himself he wouldn't have anything to worry about.

Damn Brin for burrowing under his skin, worming her way into his heart and wiggling into his soul. Brin, damn her, yanked feelings—good, bad and ugly—to the surface and made him not only confront them but also face who he was, to question what he was doing with his life.

As Radd pulled up to the lodge, his phone dinged with an incoming message. He picked the device up off the flat dashboard and swiped his finger across the screen. It was a message from Digby.

Heads up: Shanna was tanning topless on my balcony and some paparazzi scumbag caught some very mild action from me. I was, mostly, dressed. Photos published online today.

Radd read the message again, trying to make sense of the words. Shanna was Digby's on-off girlfriend and an aspiring actress. And the balcony he was referring to had to be his suite at The Vane and was supposed to be access-controlled and exceptionally private.

Radd felt his blood pressure rise.

How the hell did that happen?

Not sure but suspect Shanna had something to do with setting it up.

Holy Christ.

Don't overreact, for God sake, Radd. It's not that big a deal and it comes with the territory. Oh, and Shanna and I are over, obviously.

He should bloody well hope so. Radd gripped the bridge of his nose between his thumb and forefinger and tried to push the anger away. Radd fought his instinct to fly home, demand a retraction and thump the photographer. But his younger brother was thirty-five and fully capable of fighting his own battles.

They had a right to privacy and the lack

thereof shouldn't come "with the territory," it certainly wouldn't with his. This was a great reminder of why he shouldn't make personal connections.

"Good morning, John. How are you?"

Radd looked up to see his concierge, who was about to open Brin's passenger door.

John, elderly and dignified, gave her a regal nod, but Radd saw the hint of pleasure in his eyes at her question. "I'm very well, thank you, Miss Brin. How did you enjoy The Treehouse?"

Brin's under-her-eyelashes look, directed at him, was a little audacious and a lot naughty. "It was lovely, thank you. Some bits were better than others. The food was divine. And the setting magical."

Radd ignored her flirtatious innuendo and impatiently waited for her to join him at the bottom of the stairs. Feeling irritated and off-balance, he placed his hand on her lower back to usher her up the steps leading into the reception area. He steered her toward the deck, away from where they could hear the voices of the Radebe party.

Radd saw the question in her eyes, knew

that she'd picked up on his change of mood. He felt his Adam's apple bob, tasted emotion in the back of his throat. He desperately wanted to gather her to him, bury her face in his neck and hold on tight. He wanted to make plans with her for the rest of his life, starting with not letting her go when they touched down in Cape Town tomorrow afternoon.

But because that was impossible, because he didn't trust anybody, couldn't believe in love and commitment—he refused to, love led to hurt and loss, and why would he do that to himself?—he pushed that thought away. Digby's text messages were a fantastic reminder that this was a moment out of time, not the beginning of something real, something lasting. That he could only control *his* words and actions.

It was way past time to backpedal. And to do it hard and fast.

"Are we on the same page, Brinley?" he demanded.

Brin frowned, obviously confused. "I don't understand."

"We had sex last night—" he couldn't call

it making love; that was too intimate "—but nothing has changed between us. This can't go anywhere."

Brin blanched at his harsh tone, the softness in her eyes fading. Then, needing to put some distance between her and the verbal blow he'd dealt her, she stepped away from him. Hurt jumped into her eyes but he couldn't let her feelings distract him.

They were on a runaway train and he had to hit the brakes, to stop this madness in its tracks.

"Excuse me?"

Radd raked his hands through his hair. "You, us, nothing is going to happen when we get back home. I hope you know that."

Brin took another step back as pain settled on her face and in her eyes. He noticed a faint tremble to her chin and her suddenly pale face. Too hard and too bold, Radd cursed himself, fighting the urge to apologize. No, he was being cruel to be kind, she had to know that whatever was bubbling between them would expire in less than twenty-four hours.

Then she straightened her shoulders, pushed

steel into her spine and her eyes met his. Brin's unexpected and withering glare made him feel two feet tall. But before she could respond, Naledi called his name. For once, it was a welcome interruption.

"Your tribe awaits, my lord."

Radd didn't appreciate Brin's sarcasm.

"Radd! Look who arrived while you were away!"

Radd turned and saw Naledi, wearing an eye-poppingly brief bikini and nothing else, standing a few feet from him, her arms around the waist of her fiancé Johnathan Wolf. It took all of Radd's willpower to pull a welcoming smile onto his face, to hold out his hand for the groom to shake. Radd then turned to Brin and placed a hand on her back, silently urging her stiff body forward.

"Johnathan, meet Brinley Riddell."

"Oh, Brin and I know each other," Johnathan cheerfully replied. "But I didn't realize you were acquainted with Radd, Brinley."

Radd turned to look at Brin, watching as the last of her color faded from her face.

Oh, God...what now?

"And how do you know Brinley, Jon?" Naledi demanded in that hard-as-hell voice that made Radd, uncharacteristically, want to run for cover.

"She's Kerry Riddell's sister, darling."

Judging by Naledi's harsh scream and Brin's white-as-a-ghost face, her being Kerry's sister was, in Naledi's world, the equivalent of a plague of locusts or a runaway groom.

This… Radd gripped the bridge of his nose and squeezed.

This was why he hated secrets and surprises. And personal connections. And why he kept his distance from people.

A few hours ago she'd been lying in Radd's strong arms, completely at ease in her nakedness, exploring what it meant to give and receive pleasure. They'd made love over and over—three times? Four?—and with each pass she'd grown bolder, more confident in her power as a woman, tapping into that age-old power to make a man burn and squirm.

Radd had taken her to new sexual heights, far beyond what she'd experienced and even more than she'd imagined. In between their bouts of lovemaking, they'd talked, swapping stories about their childhoods, their favorite places, foods and movies.

Despite knowing that Radd wasn't interested in a relationship, his this-is-only-sex reminder—so blunt!—had thrown her. Had she been hoping, wondering, dreaming for more?

Maybe. Just very little. Well, no more.

Besides, she had a bigger problem to deal with right now.

Once or twice she'd thought about telling Radd about Kerry, about her feud with Naledi, but the time had never quite seemed right and she'd known it would shift the dynamic between them and, frankly, she hadn't wanted what they had to end. Not just yet. She'd thought there would be time, at the lodge or back in Cape Town—or never—for the full truth.

It seemed that time was now.

Brin closed her eyes and wondered why Johnathan, not the brightest spark in an electrical storm, remembered her—the younger sister of a woman he'd slept with—when they'd so very briefly met all those years ago.

Brin opened her mouth to say hello, but

Naledi's loud screech made her take a step back. And then another.

"She's Kerry's sister? Are you freakin' kidding me?"

"Actually, she's her half sister," Johnathan replied. "She's Kerry's personal assistant."

"I *was* her assistant," Brin corrected him, only to realize that nobody was listening to her. Brin looked past Naledi's furious face to see that the rest of the wedding party had moved closer, curiosity on their faces.

"What is she doing here? Did she take photos? She's only here to ruin my wedding!" Naledi's yell was accompanied by the stamping of her feet.

Brin turned her attention to Radd. His expression, as always, was impassive, but his eyes reflected worried confusion, like he was trying to find his balance in a suddenly rough sea.

Brin expected him to try and placate Naledi, to do or say anything to calm the drama queen down because, sure, keeping Naledi calm was imperative. But she never, not in her craziest dreams, expected his next question.

And it rocked her off her feet. "What have

you done to upset Naledi?" Radd demanded, his question whipping her skin.

Of course, it follows that this would be my fault, Brin thought, when her shock receded. She was the easiest person to blame: it didn't matter that he'd needed a florist at the last minute, that she'd begged him to take her back to Cape Town, that she'd done everything she could to avoid the Radebes.

Blame had to be assigned, and she was a convenient target. It was unfair but it wasn't, knowing the world he operated in, an uncommon practice.

"She's Kerry's sister, probably sent here to infiltrate my celebrations, to take photographs of me in wretched and compromising situations. Or when I'm looking awful," Naledi shouted.

Oh, seriously? Get over yourself!

"She came here to do the flowers, Naledi. She's a florist," Radd said, sounding annoyed.

"She did my flowers? Are you freaking kidding me? She's a nobody! I knew I hated them, didn't I tell you that I hated them?" Naledi demanded, looking around at her entourage. A couple of the bridesmaids nodded, as did her father. Her mother averted her head and said nothing.

Brin looked at Radd, waiting for him to defend her work. He'd told her numerous times that Naledi loved the flowers and would like to use her again. She held her breath, waiting for him to say something, anything.

When Radd remained quiet, Brin felt like he'd yanked her heart out of her chest and shoved it into a blast chiller. *Come on, Radd, say something... Did our fight yesterday morning teach you nothing? Did you hear me when I told you about being in the line of fire for things I had no control over? Did anything resonate with you?*

Obviously not, because Radd, damn him, remained quiet. But Naledi did not. "I demand you search her phone! I want to see if she has any unauthorized photographs of me, and if she does I will sue her for invading my privacy."

Good luck with that, Brin thought. She didn't have any money anyway. As far as she knew, Radd still hadn't paid her and, judging by his cold, hard, icy fury, he might not.

I abhor secrets and surprises...

"Naledi wants her phone inspected," Vincent stated, stepping forward and placing his hand on his daughter's shoulder.

But this was where Radd would draw the line, he knew she would never do anything to jeopardize his deal. He knew—he had to!— that she'd never do anything so underhand, that she didn't care enough about Naledi or her wedding to ruin it. He'd say no, because he knew her and he'd stand up for her.

Naledi's fist rested on her curvy hips. "I have an exclusive deal with a magazine and if a single image hits the internet before they get the package of photos, I will lose the deal and a huge paycheck."

Brin ignored her, keeping her eyes on Radd's face. *C'mon, Radd, any time now.*

His eyes, as cold as a dark, Arctic night, met hers. Brin held her breath and when he lifted his hand, she thought, for one brief, beautiful moment, that he was offering his protection, a silent but powerful gesture to show she had his support. She started to put her hand in his and gasped when he jerked his back, quick enough to avoid a snake bite.

"Can I see your phone, Ms. Riddell?"

His words took some time to sink in and when they did, Brinley stared at him, feeling hot and cold and utterly alone. She'd grown up as the outsider, constantly looking in, but she'd never felt so abandoned. A cold, wet, sharp wind sliced through her. "You want to see my phone? Why?"

Don't do this, Radd, please.

Radd just stared at her, his hand up, waiting. "This awful scene will be over a lot quicker if you comply."

Brin felt the scrape of a sob in her throat, the burn of tears. Yep, last night meant nothing. She, and her feelings, meant even less. Tossing her head, she gathered her emotions and forced them down, refusing to let Radd or any of the wedding party see her cry. Pulling her phone out of the back pocket of her jeans, she slapped it into his palm. Sucking in some much-needed air, she forced herself to look at Naledi, at Johnathan, Mr. Radebe and finally back at Radd.

Her heart was breaking, but her pride was still intact. Thank God something was.

"Go for it. But you won't find any photos of Naledi or anyone else on the device, because

I don't care." She forced herself to meet Naledi's eyes, flat and dark. "I don't care how many Instagram followers you have, about your wedding or your dress or your family. I don't have any social media accounts but, sure, feel free to check."

Radd's fingers closed around her phone and when Naledi reached to take it from him, he jerked it out of her reach. "I'm the only one who looks at this phone," he growled.

Much too little and far too late, Tempest-Vane.

Brin didn't care; he could inspect her phone, so could everyone there. It didn't matter anymore. "Feel free to keep the device," Brin told Radd, her voice brittle. "I'm going to the room to pack up my stuff. I expect to be on a flight out of here shortly or, by God, I will walk."

"Can I explain?"

Out of the corner of her eye, Brin saw Radd drop down into the seat opposite her, his big frame blocking out the soft leather as he fastened his seat belt. Brin briefly met his eyes before looking out of the plane's window. Far below Radd's fancy jet, the city of Cape Town lay nestled between the mountains and the sea.

He's taken his time to approach me, Brin thought; his jet was making its descent and within minutes they would be on the ground. Brin did not doubt Radd had timed it this way to minimize their confrontation. That was fine with her, there wasn't much to say.

She loved him, he didn't love or trust her. Simple, really.

She couldn't wait to get back to her cottage, to what was familiar. Abby's unwavering friendship, her soft bed, being able to cry into her own pillow.

But, at some point, she had to put her feelings and tumultuous emotions aside and start to think. In fact, moving her attention to her future was easier than nursing her battered and bruised heart.

She didn't want to leave Cape Town—she loved it—but how could she stay in the same city Radd did? And how could she take his now-tainted wad of cash? If she did, and established her flower shop, every time she walked inside she'd be reminded of Radd and this crazy, confusing time where she fell in love with, and had her heart broken by, him.

She'd done a job, fulfilled her end of the business arrangement and she deserved that cash, her sensible, business brain argued. What's the option here? To stay poor and to struggle?

Or to go back to Johannesburg with her tail tucked between her legs?

Her pride wanted her to make the grand gesture, to tell him to go to hell and take his money with him, but if she did that, she'd be in a worse position than she was before. Going back to work for Kerry was the second of two very bad choices...

If only you didn't have to go and fall in love with the man, Riddell, how stupid are you? He was unemotional, driven, rude and single-minded and falling for him was properly idiotic. Really, she needed someone to save her from herself.

"I told the Radebes that there were no photos on your phone."

Of course there weren't. And she so didn't care.

Radd placed his ankle on his opposite knee.

Brin allowed her eyes to wander over him: he still sported heavy, sexy stubble, but he'd changed into a pair of dark brown chinos and pulled on an aqua-colored linen, button-down shirt. His cuffs were rolled back and he wore a different watch from the high tech, too-many-buttons-to-count one he'd been wearing earlier. This watch was simple, timeless, gorgeous.

He was back to being the beautifully dressed billionaire while she was still dressed in the same clothes she'd been wearing when she left The Treehouse. Brin felt underdressed and a little gauche. Damn him for making her feel less than, for making her feel like she did when she was the tiny, unimportant moon circling Kerry's glowing planet.

"You're really angry."

Well, duh. Sure, she was furious with him, but she also felt hurt, sad and so very tired of being on the outside looking in. She'd lived on the edge of her family's circle all her life and she just wanted her own spot to shine, somewhere where she was celebrated and loved. Someone to take her side, someone to stand in her corner.

Radd, as he'd demonstrated earlier, wasn't that person. She'd never find the peace she craved with him, within the world he inhabited.

"Rich people and celebrities expect privacy, Brinley," Radd quietly stated.

"I worked for my sister as her assistant for a long time, so that's not something you need to tell me," Brin told him, ice in her voice. "I managed a lot of her PR and I understand how the game is played. I don't like the rules, but I understand them. Apart from the fact that I'm not remotely interested in Naledi and her wedding, I would never invade her privacy like that. I thought you understood that much about me."

"How could I when you didn't tell me the truth about who you are and who your sister is!" Radd raked his hand through his hair. "I asked if there was anything I should know, anything that could ruin this week."

"I was under no obligation to disclose that information to you, or anyone else, Radd. And you're using it as an excuse to push me away."

Radd's eyes narrowed at her accusation. "What?"

Brin felt the shudder of the jet's wheels touching the runway, the change in the sound of the engines as the plane slowed. "And if that doesn't work, you're going to throw in how important it is that you acquire a signed signature for the purchase of the mine, and I've put that in jeopardy. You are not your name or your company!" Brin said, feeling like she'd gone ten rounds with a champion boxer.

"You don't understand what it was like living with parents like mine!" Radd whipped back. "They dragged our name through the mud. They sold every asset my grandfather and great-grandfathers acquired, and Digby and I had to work our fingers to the bone to reclaim what was lost!"

"Everyone has a past, Radd. I grew up in the shadow of my sister. Nothing I ever did, or said, could match the brilliance and the beauty that is Kerry. But I keep reminding myself that my past is exactly that, my past, and shouldn't be allowed to color or inform my decisions. Besides, I have no interest in being with a man who puts money and business first, someone who can't stand up for, or defend, me."

Radd leaned forward and that impassive, inscrutable expression and his blank eyes told her she was dealing with Cape Town Radd, not Kagiso Radd. The Radd he was in the city was hard and unyielding, dogmatic and determined. She'd lost the man she loved, he'd been devoured by this hard-eyed man sitting across from her.

Brin lifted her phone off her thigh and swiped her thumb across the screen. Pulling in a deep breath, she gathered her courage and turned the screen to him. His eyes widened at the picture he saw on her screen.

"We became friends, Radd, and then we became lovers and our connection scares the pants off you. From the moment you rolled out of bed at The Treehouse, I could feel you retreating, your mind going a hundred miles a minute, trying to find a way to put some distance between us. And then I found this picture of Digby and his girlfriend online—"

"How?"

Brin shrugged. "I saw the photo on your phone."

"Snooping, too?" Radd muttered, frowning.

"Our seats weren't that far apart." Brin handed him an I'll-fry-you-where-you-sit glare. "And you're being petty." Brin dropped her hand and continued to speak. "But it did make all the pieces fall into place."

"Good for you."

Brin ignored his sarcastic interruption. "This photograph of Digby's girlfriend reminded you that you can't trust people, that you mustn't let anyone get too close to you. That scene with Naledi confirmed it. You *wanted* an excuse to push me away, Radd. You were desperate for one, because you are too scared to love, too scared to take a chance, too scared to go there, probably because your parents, the people who are supposed to love you the most, didn't and constantly disappointed you."

Radd released a choking sound, but Brin didn't give him the chance to speak. "And boy, you quickly found those reasons you were looking for. Do you really believe a PR campaign and a rehabilitation of your name process is going to bring you the peace you require? It's not. Because until you believe you are more than your name, until you embrace who you are, fully and without reservation, and give yourself credit for the man you've become—hard-working, intelligent, trustworthy—it's all just smoke and mirrors. You're not trying to convince the world, Radd, you're trying to convince yourself."

Brin saw the color drain from Radd's face, knew that he wanted to argue, but she held up her hand, silently asking him to be quiet.

"I kept telling myself that I'm not from your world, that I don't fit in there, but the truth is, you don't fit into *my* world, Radd. And it's got nothing to do with money and power and celebrity and…stuff. I need the people in my world to have my back, as I would have theirs. I need trust and comfort and support, someone who is prepared to build me up, not tear me down. Someone who will let me love them and love me back."

Brin placed her fist over her mouth, silently cursing the tears running down her face. "I deserve to have someone love me like that,

Radd, I do. I'm sorry it couldn't be you, but there it is."

The plane rolled to a stop and Brin saw Skye standing in the doorway of the lounge. She dredged up a smile for him, unclipped her seatbelt and stood up. She looked down at Radd, who was staring at his hands, his expression, as usual, implacable.

"Don't bother about getting me home, Radd. I contacted Abby and she's collecting me. It's been…" Brin hesitated. Lovely? Exciting? Soul-touching? Devastating? They all applied so she settled on "…interesting."

"Goodbye, Radd."

Brin forced herself to walk away and kept her eyes on the open door and the steps she had to walk down. She was furiously angry with him, hurt and disappointed that he wasn't brave enough to love her, but his faults and actions didn't dilute her love for him. He was the puzzle piece she'd been looking for all her life to complete her, the part of her soul she was missing. He was her shelter in the storm, her soft place to fall.

Radd, the man and not the image, was whom she wanted to be with, the face she woke up to every morning, the body she cuddled up against at night. The person she wanted to laugh with, love with, make babies with.

But she couldn't do any of that on her own; it took two to have a once-in-a-lifetime love affair. He didn't know it but Radd, scared and a little lost, held her heart in his hands.

Hot tears ran as Brin realized that, from this moment on, she'd have to learn to live without both.

CHAPTER TEN

"You don't fit into my world..."

"I need the people in my world to have my back."

"Someone who will let me love them and love me back."

"Goddammit, Radd, sit still!"

Seated in the back row, Radd ignored his brother's hiss and watched Naledi flash a practiced smile at the professional cameraman as Johnathan slid his ring onto her finger and murmured "I do."

Shouldn't she be looking at her groom, immersed in the moment of tying herself to another person, reveling in their love and good fortune? Shouldn't she be paying more attention to Johnathan than she did to the camera?

"Six months," Digby murmured.

Radd turned his head to look at his brother. "What?"

"I give them six months before they start

talking divorce. They'll be single in, mmm, maybe nine." Digby shrugged at his surprised look. "I've seen so many brides stroll through the doors of The Vane, but I've never seen one so into herself as Naledi Radebe. There's only space in that relationship for one person and she's it."

"Brin said something similar." God, even murmuring her name hurt. Why? She was never going to be part of his life. No one was.

And if that was true then why did he spend the last thirty-six hours talking himself out of going to her, calling her? Radd rubbed his chest somewhere in the region of his heart and wondered if it would ever stop aching.

Maybe he was having a heart attack or something. Or maybe he was just missing Brin.

"I need trust and comfort and support..."

He wasn't capable of giving her what she needed.

"Did you see the letter we received from our parent's lawyer?" Digby asked out of the side of his mouth. "The beneficiary of their trust wants to meet us, on certain conditions."

Right now, he really didn't care. And he

wasn't even remotely curious who Gil and Zia had left their money to. How to heal the crater-sized hole Brin had left in his life was taking up all his mental energy.

"Brin is Kerry Riddell's sister," Radd whispered the words in Digby's ear.

"Did you hear what I said? About meeting whomever they left their assets to?"

"Mmm. Brin told me I'm living in the past and that the PR campaign is just a way to convince myself I am better than them."

Digby released an under-his-breath curse and closed his eyes. Then he pushed his way to his feet and, when Radd looked up at him, jerked his head. Radd got the message and slowly climbed to his feet, thankful they were in the back of many, many rows and could slip away without disturbing the wedding.

The brothers walked in silence to the open-air bar set up on the magnificent veranda a good distance from the wedding gazebo. Digby walked behind the counter and reached for a bottle of whiskey and two glasses. After pouring a healthy amount into both glasses, he handed Radd his tumbler before speaking again. "Your florist is Kerry's sister? BS."

"Do you know Kerry Riddell?" Radd asked, after taking a healthy belt of his drink. He welcomed the burn, and then the warmth, hitting his stomach. It was the first time he'd felt anything but ice cold since Brin left him on the plane.

"Yeah, we've met. She's a piece of work."

Needing to talk, a surprising development in itself, Radd rolled the tumbler between the palms of his hands. "I only found out Brin's connection to her when Johnathan told Naledi she was Kerry's sister at Kagiso. Naledi did not take the news well."

"Bet she lost her rag and accused Brin of trying to spoil her wedding."

Radd placed his glass on the bar and started pacing the area in front of Digby. Six steps, turn. Ten steps, turn again. "Good guess."

Digby grinned. "Not that good, because Mari told me. She also told me that you are into Brin."

Radd snorted, stopped and took another sip of his whisky. "We had a brief fling and it's over." He started to pace again. "It was… inconsequential."

Radd looked up at the clear sky, watching

for a stray lightning bolt to punish him for that enormous lie.

"Sure it was," Digby mocked him. "That's why you barely reacted when I told you about the heir to the trust, why you brushed that news off to focus on a florist. Face it, Radd, she is your person."

Radd stopped abruptly, whirled around and scowled at his brother. "Are you looking to get thumped? You know how I feel about settling down, about marrying!"

"I do," Digby replied, obviously amused.

"Then why would you make such an asinine comment?" Radd demanded, resuming his pacing.

"You're shouting. And you are pacing."

Radd threw his hands up in frustration at Digby's observation. There was no one around, no guests to be disturbed, so what was his problem?

Digby chuckled at his question, and Radd's hands curled into tight fists. *No hitting your younger brother, even if he deserves it.* "What the hell is so damn funny?"

"You! Look at you, all pissed off and pacing. I haven't seen you this worked up in…

well, forever. You are the most impassive, nonreactive person I know, yet here you are, all tied up in a knot over a woman."

Radd wanted to argue but couldn't because, from the first moment he'd met her, Brin had the ability to shove her hand into his soul and pull all his dormant emotions to the surface. Radd scrubbed his hands over his face, his anger fading. He sent Digby a rueful look. "She drives me nuts."

"And that's a very good thing," Digby replied.

"Not from my perspective," Radd grumbled.

Digby smiled, picked up his drink and swirled it around before speaking again. "Since Jack's death, you have tended to be a little..."

"A little what?" Radd prompted him when Digby hesitated.

"Robotic." Digby shrugged. "Look, when Jack died, we had to grow up, and we did, fast. We had to deal with the parents, the gossip around them and the loss of our legacy. In our drive to regain what was lost, we also, to an extent, lost ourselves."

"Explain," Radd commanded, his throat dry. This conversation wouldn't be easy, but it was long overdue. The path they were on, which had seemed so clear a week or so ago, was now shrouded in fog.

"We both changed after Jack died, in fundamental ways. We worshipped Jack, he was our hero, our anchor point. And the parent's betrayal knocked us sideways, and them returning to their hedonistic lifestyle so soon after his death was another blow."

"Maybe that was the way they coped with his death," Radd suggested, shocked by this new insight.

"Maybe. Or maybe you are giving them too much credit," Digby said, his eyes stormy. "Anyway, as I was saying, Jack's death changed everything. You became an adult overnight and I became a rebel. God, it was a miracle I managed to finish school without being kicked out."

Only because he'd gone to the headmaster and begged him to let Digby stay in school. But Radd didn't tell Dig that, he didn't need to know.

"I acted out, looking for a way to ease the

pain, but you internalized everything and cultivated this nothing-can-hurt-me persona." Digby jammed his hands into the pockets of his suit pants, his eyes sober. "I, mostly, grew out of my rebellious stage, but you kept your hard-as-nails facade. I'm not going to lie, it worries me. That's why I am so damn happy that you've found someone to make you feel."

Brin did. Make him feel, that is. He still didn't like it.

But he couldn't deny it. Around Brin, he felt both relaxed and energized, calm and excited. He felt normal...

"Brin seems to think that I'm using the PR campaign to make me feel better about myself," Radd admitted. Digby was the only person he could discuss this with, he'd walked this path with him. And until he figured out whether she was right or wrong, or a mixture of both, he was paralyzed.

He wanted to move on. How and where to, he had no idea, but he wasn't the type to stand still and do nothing.

Digby stared at a point past Radd's shoulder, and Radd knew he was looking at the superb view of Table Mountain. Digby's opinion on Brin's accusation was important, and he was very willing to wait.

Dig's eyes eventually met his. "She's right, Radd, you and I both know it. I don't blame us for trying to restore the company to what it was, it gave two very messed-up kids a goal, a direction we so badly needed. But I'm not, as I've mentioned, a fan of the PR campaign, I feel we'd be beating a dead horse. People will think what they think and we know the truth. And maybe we should move forward without thinking about how the world perceives us."

Digby didn't, and never had, cared what people thought about him. He marched to the beat of his own drum and people could either like it or lump it.

Radd felt like the world was shifting below his feet. Everything that seemed so stable a week ago was now shaky, everything he firmly believed in felt less substantial.

All because a silver-eyed siren flipped his life upside down and inside out.

"Noted." Radd made himself ask the question. "Should we still go ahead with acquiring the mine?"

"Absolutely." Digby nodded. "You survived the pre-wedding week at Kagiso and by now the bride and groom should be hitched and stitched, so why not? Get Vincent to sign the sale agreement and let's get it done. Once the mine is in our hands, we can decide on the PR campaign and where we want to take the company without any pressure from the past. Though I think you should be working out how to get Brin back in your life. It's obvious that you are head-over-ass in love with her."

No, he wasn't! Radd sent Digby a hot look and noticed Dig's eyebrows rising, as if daring him to disagree. He wanted to... He should.

He liked Brin, and adored her body. Sex with her was magical and he loved spending time with her, but that didn't mean he loved her...

Digby flashed him an evil grin. "If you aren't in love with her, then I might track her down and ask her out."

A red mist formed behind Radd's eyes and it took all his willpower not to put his hands around Digby's throat and squeeze. Brin was his.

"Do it and die."

Digby's expression turned mocking, then amused. "Just get over yourself and admit it already, brother."

Aargh!

Okay, yes, maybe he was in love with her. But who fell in love in under a week? Could he trust his feelings, as new and strange as they were? Radd, with considerable effort, pushed aside his fears and, after taking a deep breath, examined his feelings for Brin.

She made him feel whole, complete, the best version of himself. He loved her dirty laugh, her sexy smile, the sway of her hips and the way she crinkled her nose when she was deep in thought.

Nothing else, not the mine, not the business, not even Digby, mattered as much as she did; he was now second in his own life. Brin was all that was important.

He couldn't live his life, didn't want to, without her. *Melodramatic much, Tempest-Vane?* It was hard to admit, but having Brin in his life would enrich it exponentially, far more than the money in his bank accounts had ever been able to do.

She was all that mattered, all that was important.

"Ah, and the penny has dropped," Digby commented, his tone smug.

Radd managed a small smile. Then he winced. "It's all very well me having a come-to-Jesus moment, but that doesn't mean that she'll have me."

"Nope, she'd be mad to take you on. I'm a far better bet," Digby teased.

Radd's "screw you" held no heat. Digby laughed and then his expression turned guarded. Radd turned to see who'd caught his attention and saw Vincent Radebe strolling across the vibrant, immaculate lawn toward them. That meant that the wedding was over.

Radd remembered that the wedding party was supposed to gather by the whimsical fountain for photographs and wondered why Vincent had left the wedding party. Naledi would not be pleased.

The guests wouldn't be far behind him so if Radd wanted to slip away—he couldn't wait to track Brin down—he needed to leave soon.

Vincent held up his hand in a "wait, please" gesture and Radd frowned, not bothering to hide his impatience.

"I'm having second thoughts about selling the mine," Vincent said, folding his arms across his chest.

Now why didn't that surprise him? Radd waited for the wave of anger, the crashing waves of disappointment. Neither arrived. Interesting...

Before he could respond, Digby, looking cool, urbane but very, very determined, met Vincent's gaze. "That's your prerogative, of course. Now, if you'd be so kind as to accompany me to the accounts office, I will need your credit card to pay for this wedding at our usual rate. " He turned to Radd. "Shall I add the cost of the wedding party's stay at Kagiso, as well?"

If he was backpedaling on their agreement then they'd make him pay. Nobody pushed the Tempest-Vane brothers around. Not anymore and not ever again.

"Absolutely. Vincent's guests enjoyed the full package at Kagiso."

Vincent's deep brown skin paled. "Uh..."

"Thank you for allowing us to host one of the most iconic, and expensive weddings of the past ten years at The Vane," Digby said, still using that smooth voice. "We are honored and grateful. I'm afraid the bill might sting, but that's the price for lifelong memories."

Radd almost snorted. Naledi and Johnathan wouldn't last the year, never mind a lifetime. "How much are we looking at?" Vincent asked, sounding a little choked up.

"More than a million," Digby suavely replied. "Maybe a million and a half."

"And that's including the stay at Kagiso?"

Radd shook his head. "No, that's just the cost of the wedding. Your cost to stay at Kagiso will probably be another million."

Vincent swore and he rubbed his hand over his bald head. *Yeah, you tight-fisted, bastard*, Radd thought, *we don't play.*

Radd was over playing games with him, was tired of being the puppet dancing as Vincent pulled the strings. It wasn't who he was; he didn't like it and it was time to end this farce. He was tired of paying for his parent's mistakes.

"Look Vincent, we all know you want to sell the mine, it's no secret that you are focusing on telecommunications. You've held on to the mine, probably because it is so damn profitable. We've made you a solid offer and we threw in hosting this wedding, and your stay at Kagiso, at cost. You want to sell the mine, but you're hoping you can squeeze some more cash out of us. It's been fun making Gil's sons dance, you've enjoyed a little payback."

He saw the flash of agreement in the older man's eyes.

"It's not going to work," Radd informed him. "The game stops, here. *Today.*"

"But everyone knows that the mine is the missing piece of the Tempest-Vane empire." Vincent threw his argument back in his face.

Radd caught Digby's eye and his brother nodded, handing him his full support. They could live without the mine, and they would. Brin was right, this was about *stuff*, other people's perceptions and, at the end of the day, not *that* important. The world wouldn't stop turning if the mine wasn't added to the group and, since he knew he wasn't like his father—or his mother—did the rehabilitation of their name matter?

If he took a wife, she might care, but Brin was the only person he could imagine in that role. And she *definitely* didn't care.

God, he loved her. Radd hauled in a deep breath and realized that the boulder that usually lived on his chest was gone. So this was what freedom felt like. He rather liked it.

"It's a business, Vincent, not a lifesaving organ transplant. Sell us the mine, as per our original agreement, or don't. Either way, we'll be fine," Radd told him. He nodded to the wave of guests heading their way, led by the harassed-looking wedding planner.

"You need to join your family, Vincent," Radd told him.

Vincent glanced at the wedding planner and sighed. "Don't you want to know what I've decided?"

"I don't care," he told Vincent, knowing it was the truth. "Frankly, I've got something bigger to worry about."

Digby jerked his head toward the building. "Go get her, Radd."

"Thanks, Dig."

"And if she says no, I'll pick up where you left off. I'm younger, more charming and more handsome than you."

Funny, Radd thought as he strode into the hotel. Not.

Abby held her hand as they walked up the steps leading from the beach to the parking lot, and Brin appreciated her support.

So much has happened between the last time I saw these steps last Saturday and now, Brin thought. She'd flown across the country, visited the most amazing game reserve, met Mari, fought with Naledi and, worst of all, handed her heart over to Radd.

Who didn't want it.

"Brin!" Abby snapped her fingers in front of her face. She'd been doing that a lot since Brin had arrived back home yesterday afternoon. She'd been a wreck, and Abby had taken her in her arms, pulled her into their house and let her cry. Then she poured them huge glasses of wine and pulled every excruciating detail out of Brin.

And today, on finding Brin still in bed at noon, she'd pushed her into the shower and then bundled her into her car, telling her that an afternoon in the sun, swimming in the sea, would make her feel so much better.

Brin was still waiting for that to happen.

She still felt utterly exhausted. She'd hardly slept last night—her brain insisted on reliving every interaction with Radd over and over again, always ending with the vision of Radd's hard face on their trip home, and his scathing words *"This can't go anywhere."*

The crack in her heart widened.

"I sent you a number for my cousin, he's a real estate agent and he's trying to find a florist shop owner who might sell. He's also looking for vacant shops for you to consider."

"I don't think I can take Radd's money, Abby," Brin quietly stated.

How could she explain that it all meant nothing without Radd? That if she was feeling like this, like the shell of the person she once was, she had no interest in establishing a business, and that she might as well go back to Johannesburg and work for Kerry. Her hell-on-wheels sister couldn't make her feel any worse than she currently did.

"I know that this is difficult but you have to

think with your head, not your heart," Abby replied, squeezing her hand. "Give it a few weeks before you make any radical decisions about returning his money. You're hurt and upset and you don't want to make a huge decision when you are feeling emotional."

It was a solid piece of advice, but Brin knew she wouldn't take it. As soon as the money hit her account—it was still looking as empty as ever—she'd ask Abby for his bank account number; she was his employee after all. If Abby didn't know it or couldn't get it, she would contact Radd.

Going back to Johannesburg wouldn't be *that* bad—it was, after all, what she knew. She'd have a good salary, a decent car to drive, financial security. And after having her heart broken by Radd—her fault for thinking that she could capture his attention and his love—her sister's and mother's snubs, criticism and demands wouldn't have the power to wound her.

They would be like the gentle flick of a whip compared to being eviscerated by a blunt teaspoon.

Stupid girl for allowing this to happen, for

not guarding your heart. For falling into the arms of a man who she knew was so very far out of her league. *Never again*, Brin vowed.

She was done with men and love.

Permanently.

"Brin…"

Brin lifted her head to look at her friend as she stepped onto the pavement at the top of the steps. She knew that Abby meant well, but she just wanted a little peace, some time to nurse her broken heart, her bruised spirit. She needed time to recover, to mourn what could've been.

"Can you just leave me be, Abs? I'm tired and sad—" Abby's hand shot out and her fingernails dug into the bare skin on her arm. Abby was looking to her right, and Brin followed her gaze.

Radd.

Brin drank him in, all six-foot-something of him, dressed in a lightweight grey suit, his tie pulled down from his collar, leaning against the hood of his fancy car. He'd been to Naledi's wedding, Brin dimly remembered, but he must've left shortly after the ceremony was done. Why wasn't he at the reception and, more importantly, why was he here?

Radd straightened, sliding his hands into the pockets of his suit pants. Aviator sunglasses covered his eyes and he looked as he always did, implacable and remote.

Nothing has changed, Brin thought. So, instead of walking over to him, she turned and walked in the direction of Abby's car. She heard Abby behind her, hurrying to keep up with her long-legged stride.

"Talk to him, Brin!" Abby pleaded.

"There's nothing to say," Brin replied, tugging on the handle to the passenger door. "I'm begging you, Abby, take me home."

"I'll just follow you there," Radd said from behind her. "We need to talk, Brin."

Brin spun around, anger temporarily drowning her sadness. "I think we covered all the bases yesterday, Mr. Tempest-Vane."

Radd winced. "Yesterday I was being a bloody idiot. Today, hopefully, I'm less of one."

"Doubtful," Brin snapped.

"Come home with me, Brin. Let's try and sort this out!"

"There's nothing to sort out," Brin told him, her voice rising.

"Now, that's a lie," Radd replied. "We have a lot to discuss and you know it." Radd turned his attention to Abby and gave her a small smile. "Go on home, Abby, I'll drive Brin to wherever she wants to go later."

Brin narrowed her eyes at Abby. "Don't you dare leave me, Abigail."

Abby shrugged. "He's my boss, Brin. And he'll fire me if I don't do as he says." She raised her eyebrows at Radd. "Won't you?"

"Damn straight." Radd soberly answered.

Did they think she was stupid? Radd wouldn't fire Abby for such a trivial reason, and they both knew it. No, she was being maneuvered into having a conversation with Radd and she didn't like it. Frustrated with both of them, she threw up her hands and pulled out her phone.

"Fine, I'll call for a taxi or an Uber."

Radd moved quickly, and she caught a hint of his cologne as her phone was yanked from her hand. Radd tucked it into the inside pocket of his jacket and folded his arms.

"You and I are going to talk," Radd told her before shoving his sunglasses into the inside pocket of his jacket. "Go, Abby."

Brin heard Abby's car door opening, followed by her engine starting, but she couldn't pull her eyes off Radd's. With dark stripes under his red eyes, he looked like he'd had even less sleep than her. His olive complexion was pale in the late afternoon light.

But his eyes, God, his eyes…

She could see a hundred emotions in those inky eyes: fear, regret, pain. It was as if he'd stripped every layer of protection away and allowed her to step into his mind and it was, like hers, in turmoil.

Radd gestured to an empty bench that faced the sea. "I have some things I need to say and, afterwards, if nothing resonates with you, I'll take you home, no questions asked."

Brin looked around and saw Abby's car exiting the parking lot. What choice did she have? Abby was gone and, since Radd had her phone, she was out of options.

"How did you know I was here?" Brin demanded as they walked over to the bench.

"I texted Abby, she told me."

What a traitor! Her best friend had known she was about to be ambushed and she'd said nothing. They would, Brin decided, be having words later. Whose side was she on?

Radd waited until she was seated before sitting down next to her. He shed his jacket and placed it on top of her beach bag sitting on the bench between them. Rolling up the cuffs of his sleeves, he stared out to sea.

"The sea looks so inviting. Was the water warm?"

Brin rolled her eyes. He wanted to talk about the temperature of the sea? Really? "Is the water ever warm in Cape Town?" she asked, sounding acerbic.

"I can't remember when last I spent any time on a beach."

"That happens when you spend all your time at work," Brin snapped, folding her arms across her chest. She couldn't do this, it was too hard. She couldn't sit here and pretend everything was fine when she loved him so much. It was like having a blowtorch blistering her body, one painful inch at a time.

"I paid you your money this morning.

It should be in your account soon," Radd told her.

"I don't want it."

Radd released an impatient snort. "Brin, we made a deal. You worked through the night to fulfill your end of the bargain. Mine was to pay you and that's done."

"I don't *want* your money," Brin replied, sounding stubborn.

"I don't care. Our business arrangement is over," Radd replied.

Yeah, she got that message loud and clear. Why had he come all this way to tell her he'd paid her? He could've texted her or sent her an email.

God, she was exhausted and her brain felt like it was on the point of exploding.

"Please take me home, Radd," Brin begged, not caring if he heard the hint of tears in her voice.

Radd pushed his hands through his hair before turning to face her. He lifted his hand, and his thumb swiped away the one tear she hadn't managed to blink away. "Please don't cry, Brin."

"Then stop making me cry and leave me

alone!" Brin cried, placing her face in her hands.

"I can't, sweetheart," Radd's reply sounded tortured, but the hand he placed on her back was strangely reassuring. "I can't walk away from you, I don't *want* to walk away."

Brin dropped her hands, but she wasn't brave enough to look at him, so she looked at the dune grass growing in the beach sand a couple of feet away from their shoes. "That's not what you said yesterday."

"Yesterday wasn't one of my better days." Radd released a heavy sigh. His hand moved up her back to the back of her neck, which he gently held. "Won't you sit up and look at me, Brin?"

Brin reluctantly straightened, and it took quite a bit of courage to meet his eyes. This was the stripped-down version of Radd, and all his feelings were reflected in his eyes. And he was feeling quite a lot, which was odd for her implacable, once-in-a-lifetime lover.

"I treated you badly yesterday, Brinley, and for that, I beg your forgiveness," Radd quietly stated. "I should've, yet again, stood up for what was right instead of what was convenient, and I disappointed and hurt you."

He had and he did. She couldn't argue with that.

"I should've told Naledi to get lost when she demanded to see your phone, I should never have invaded your privacy like that. I should've trusted you."

Brin nodded, not quite ready to let him off the hook. "Yes, you should have."

When Radd didn't say anything for the next few minutes, Brin stood up, her heart smothered by disappointment. What had she expected? For him to tell her he loved her? Silly, silly girl.

"Now that you've got that off your chest, will you take me home? Or better yet, allow me to call for a taxi. Or a lift."

Radd took her hand and tugged her back down, his hand sending sparks over her skin, up her arm. She was still as attracted to him as ever, damn it. Why was life torturing her like this?

"I'm not done," Radd told her.

"Well, get done," Brin retorted. She couldn't take much more.

He turned to look at her, and Brin's lungs contracted at the look on his face. It was part insecurity, part hope, all fear. "I've never told someone I loved them before, so I'm bound to botch this up. Give me a sec, okay?"

What? Wait! Did he just say something about love or were her ears playing tricks on her? It was highly possible. Brin laid her hand on her chest. "What did you say?"

Radd sat up, his eyes connecting with hers. "I wanted to say this with finesse, with some sort of eloquence, but nothing, despite practicing all the way here, is coming out right. So…sod it."

He clasped her face in his hands before swiping his mouth across hers. "I'm a fool and an idiot, but I'm the fool and idiot who loves you to distraction. Oh, God, you're crying again."

Brin allowed a little laugh to escape and waved her hands in front of her face before gripping Radd's strong wrists with her shaking hands. "Can you say that again?"

Radd kissed her nose, her cheekbones and

then her temple. "I love you, Brinley. So much."

Her tears started to fall in earnest. "But, yesterday, you told me you didn't see me in your future."

Radd sighed, his breath warm against her temple. "I was scared and confused and being a jerk. I thought that the mine and my work were all that was important and I wanted to keep the status quo. Loving you is new, scary territory, a place where I have no control, and I don't like giving up control."

"So what changed between then and now?" Brin asked, leaning back so she could see his face.

Radd dropped his hands from her face but placed one hand on her bare thigh, as if he needed to anchor himself to her. He looked away briefly before facing her again. "I had a conversation with Digby. He said that I was acting like a cat on a hot tin roof and wanted to know why I wasn't being my calm, distant self.

"Since I met you, I've felt more than ever before, certainly more since Jack died. The world seems a little brighter, a lot more colorful." Radd winced, looking embarrassed. "God, that sounds too cheesy for words. As I said, this is all coming out wrong."

Brin shook her head, her heart slowly defrosting. "No, every word is perfect. Carry on."

"You want more?" Radd pulled a face at her.

"No, I want everything," Brin softly told him. "Don't hold back, Radd. I've never had anyone tell me they love me before, so feel free to go overboard."

Radd's thumb stroked her cheekbone. "Oh, sweetheart, I intend to make you feel ridiculously loved every day for the rest of your life. You, not the mine, not my work, not my brother, are now my priority, and making sure you are happy is my biggest goal. I want you to have the money, not only because that was the deal, but also because I want you to have your dream. You are so talented, and I want you to open your florist-and-coffee shop."

Brin's nose wrinkled, her expression doubtful. "You'd support me in that?"

"Sure. You're far too bright and talented to sit at home, waiting for me to finish work.

No, chase your dreams, Brin and I'll support you as you do that." Radd's thumb traced the soft skin of her bottom lip. "I am so sorry I made you feel unimportant when you are everything that's important to me."

Brin bit her lip, looking up at him through her lashes. "Really?"

"Yes, *really*."

Brin stared at him, trying to compute his words, struggling to make sense of the bright, sparkly, glitter-tinged feelings coursing through her. Radd loved her.

Radd. Loved. Her.

Holy cupcakes. With sprinkles on them.

"Will you please say something?" Radd growled.

Brin saw the impatience in his eyes and decided to tease him, just a little. "What do you want me to say?"

"Well, an 'I love you' would be nice. And a 'Yes, I'll marry you, as soon as you like,' would be better."

He wants to marry me? Whoa! Really? Brin felt her heart leave her chest and take flight. *Well, okay then.*

"You haven't asked me to marry you," Brin

284 HOW TO UNDO THE PROUD BILLIONAIRE

pointed out, just managing to hold back her huge grin and her bubbling laughter.

"I will, as soon as you tell me that you love me too," Radd replied, sounding a little cross.

"Who falls in love in a week?" Brin mused. "It's crazy."

"I do, and I hope you have too or else I'm going to feel like an even bigger fool," Radd muttered. Brin heard the note of anxiety in his voice and knew that it wasn't fair to push him any further. Because, like her, he'd lived without love for a long time and didn't deserve to wait any longer.

"Of course I love you, Radd," Brin quietly told him, her eyes begging him to believe her. "So much."

Radd rested her forehead on hers and closed his eyes. "Thank God."

"And I am sorry about not telling you about my connection to Naledi," Brin said, resting her fingertips on his jaw, rough with stubble. "I didn't want to go back to my family with my tail between my legs. I'm sorry if being related to Kerry caused you any problems with Vincent. I don't want you to lose the mine because of something so silly."

Radd sat back but he kept her hand in his. "Vincent will either sell us the mine or he won't. Either way, I can live with it."

"But it's the company you need to restore the Tempest-Vane holdings to what they once were."

Radd shrugged. "While it would be nice, Digby and I agreed that it's not something we'll lose sleep over. In a few weeks, my brother and I will meet and we'll decide on what we want to do, without reference to the past and our parents."

Brin rested her forehead on the ball of his shoulder. "Are you sure?"

Radd's hand stroked her hair. "Very. It's time for a new chapter, Brinley. Will you help me write it?"

Brin nodded and squeezed his hand. "I will. Ask me again."

Radd tipped his head to the side, his expression puzzled. But it took just a few seconds for her words to register. And then her once hard-eyed, implacable man dropped to one knee in front of her, the late afternoon sun glinting off his dark hair.

"Brinley Riddell, will you marry me?"

Brin nodded once, then grinned. "On one condition."

Radd groaned theatrically and gently banged his head against her kneecap. "You're going to keep me on my toes, aren't you?"

Brin's laughter gurgled and bubbled as she ran her hands through his hair. "I want to get married at Kagiso and spend part of our honeymoon at The Treehouse."

"I'm sure that can be arranged. I happen to know the owner. Is that a yes?"

Brin nodded, her eyes shimmering with emotion. "Yes, that's a yes."

"I'm going to kiss the hell out of you in a second, but I should tell you that I have a condition, too," Radd murmured.

She was so happy she'd agree to anything. Brin grinned at him. "What's your condition?"

"That I buy you a new car. I refuse to allow you to drive that rust bucket anywhere," Radd told her, frowning. "It's not safe, Brin. I can't bear the thought of you not being safe."

"I was going to buy a car out of the money you paid me," Brin told him. There were different ways to say I love you and this was one of them.

"Let me do it," Radd said, looking serious.

Brin lifted a finger and pushed it into his chest. "I'll agree to something sensible and reasonable. I do not need fancy. Or expensive."

Radd bracketed her face with his hands. "Are we doing this? Getting married?" he asked, sounding a little bemused.

Brin laughed. "We are."

"Thank God. I can't wait to make you mine," Radd muttered before surging to his feet and yanking her up and into his arms. His mouth covered hers and Brin sank into his embrace, knowing that he would hold her, that she'd found her person.

She was, finally, home and standing in a bright, golden spotlight all of her own.

* * * * *

LET'S TALK

Romance

For exclusive extracts, competitions
and special offers, find us online:

f facebook.com/millsandboon

⊙ @millsandboonuk

🐦 @millsandboon

Or get in touch on 0844 844 1351*

For all the latest titles coming soon,
visit millsandboon.co.uk/nextmonth